Fun
Sensations
Sexy
Stories
Collection

VOLUME 26

10 EROTIC SHORT STORIES

FARRAH SEAGER

Fun Sensations/ Farrah Seager. -- 1st ed.
Xplicit Press, an imprint of TLM Media LLC

ISBN-13: 978-1-62327-557-0
ISBN-10: 1-62327-557-1
eISBN: 978-1-62327-607-2

Printed in the United States of America

CONTENTS

.

1 BOILING POINT

Sophie walked into her local bar and immediately looked around for her friend Tiffany. They arranged to meet in their usual place at 9. Sophie was running a little late, so she was sure that Tiff would already be there. She gazed around the room and she noticed Tiff sitting at a table towards the back of the bar. Her eyes were drawn to the brunette girl who sat next to her friend. Sophie was sure that she had never met this person before, as she was certain that she would not have forgotten such a beautiful girl.

Sophie couldn't help but let a smile creep over her face as she watched the two women throw back a shot of tequila and make the inevitable grimacing faces that followed. As the girls recovered, Sophie made her way over to them, secretly pleased that she missed this first round of shots.

"Hey Soph, there you are!" exclaimed Tiffany who suddenly noticed her friend walking towards them. "I want you to meet Emma; she's a friend of mine from work."

Emma stood up to shake Sophie's hand. As she did Sophie couldn't help but notice Emma's body was just as stunning as her face. She was wearing very short shorts that were styled with rips and tears in a number of places. This revealed the smooth flawless skin of her upper thighs. A simple white tank top covered her chest with just enough cleavage showing to suggest her breasts were a decent size. Her dark wavy hair came to a rest just below her shoulders, framing her delicate face. All of a sudden, Sophie realized that she had not so subtly been checking Emma out and had not yet uttered a word.

"Hi, I-I'm Sophie" she stuttered,

"It's nice to meet you, why don't you sit down and I'll get the next round in," Emma said. She looked Sophie straight in the eyes with a cheeky smile that caused Sophie to look away, almost blushing. As Emma walked away, Sophie couldn't help but stare at her ass and admire the way it wiggled from side to side as she walked in those tight denim shorts. None of this went un-noticed by Tiff who was watching

Sophie's every reaction with a knowing smile.

"So I take it your pleased that I brought my friend tonight?" Tiffany mocked. "You know you could be a little more subtle! And it's not like you to get tongue-tied and shy, what happened to the womanizing Sophie White?"

Sophie did have somewhat of a reputation when it came to getting the ladies. At 24, she was happy to be single and willing to make good use of the status. She was popular too and didn't usually have to work too hard to get what she wanted. Her hair was shoulder length, straight and blonde, and her pale complexion contrasted with her dark blue eyes. In her opinion, her body wasn't bad, with C cup breasts, a slim waist and a nice tight ass.

"I know, I was just surprised. I didn't know you were bringing anyone and... wow, why have you never brought her before?"

"She's new in the office. This was her first week; I thought it would be nice to bring her out and get to know her a bit," Tiff replied.

"So... what's her situation? Is she gay? Is she seeing anyone?" Sophie wanted to know, trying to keep a look of nonchalance about her as she did.

"I don't know yet, it hasn't come up.

Like I said, I've only know her a week and up until now it's been all work talk. Besides, you can ask her yourself now, she's coming back." Tiff said giving her head a little nod towards the bar.

Emma came back with two beers and three more tequila shots. This gave Sophie an indication of what kind of night this was going to be. They spoke about different things, including work and Emma's new apartment, all the while drinking several more rounds of shots. When a DJ replaced the band, the three of them had to lean in closer to hear one another. Sophie didn't mind this at all. After various trips to the bar, Emma had ended up sitting next to her. On a number of occasions, Emma's hand had grazed Sophie's thigh and she couldn't help but wonder whether or not it had been accidental. Each time it happened, Sophie felt little shocks of electricity travelling up her leg and into her pussy. She was becoming more and more turned on by this girl.

As the conversation began to get both louder and more personal, it was revealed that all three of them were single and therefore on the lookout. Sophie, who had been looking out for signs all night as to whether Emma was interested in girls or guys, decided that this was the perfect opportunity to ask straight out.

"So that means, Tiff is keeping her eyes open for a guy, I'm keeping my eyes open for a girl... and who exactly is it that you're looking for Emma?" Sophie asked, all the time maintaining eye contact with her new friend. The shyness from earlier clearly was replaced with alcohol confidence.

"You want to know who I'm looking for?" responded Emma, all the time holding Sophie's eye contact with just as much confidence and a very subtle one sided smile that made her eyes sparkle. "You will just have to wait and see!" And with that, she gave Emma's thigh a light squeeze, stood up and walked over to the dance floor.

"Come on, let's go dance," Sophie called over to Tiffany.

"Nah that's alright, I want to go talk to Tim at the bar. He's working tonight and I haven't seen him for ages. You go and keep Emma company, I know you want to!"

Sophie gave her friend a smile and went to find Emma through the crowds on the dance floor. She saw her talking to some guy, one of the regulars but not someone she was on speaking terms with, and walked towards them. When Emma noticed her, she grabbed her arm frantically then turned to the man and politely said, "This is my friend, it was nice to meet you." Then Emma pulled Sophie by the arm away from the man towards the centre of the dance floor.

"Thank god, what took you so long?!" Emma complained, playfully hitting the blonde on the arm.

"Hey!" Sophie played back. She leaned close to Emma's ear so she could hear over the music, "Anyway it looked like you were doing okay. First minute on the dance floor and you get chatted up by a nice young man! Looks like your single days will soon be..."

Before she could finish her sentence, Emma had turned her head and placed a light kiss on Sophie's lips to shut her up. She looked up and into Emma's eyes and could see by the twinkle in them that she was smiling. At that moment Emma turned around and began dancing and shaking her ass up against Sophie's body. Sophie still somewhat surprised by the kiss looked down at the sexy sight and couldn't resist the urge to grab the smaller girl's hips and pull her in close. As her feet danced, her hands explored Emma's thighs and stomach, loving the feeling of her warm body. Emma too, whilst continuing to move her body was relishing in the feeling of Sophie's hands all over her body. She could feel her temperature rising and not only because of the energetic dancing. At one point as

Sophie's hands moved slowly from her thigh to her stomach, they brushed dangerously close to her pussy and Emma could feel the wetness seeping out into her underwear. With this, she turned around and leaned forward for their second kiss. Sophie closed her eyes as she revelled in the taste of Emma's sweet lip-gloss. As Emma slightly parted her lips, Sophie took the opportunity to lightly nibble on the brunette's bottom lip, causing a tingling sensation to run right through her body.

Emma brought her hands, which at some point during the kiss had found themselves holding Sophie's hips, slowly up her new friends back until one of them was in her hair, lightly holding her head to keep the pressure on the kiss. As they continued, the kiss became more passionate and both girls were becoming more forceful. Sophie's hands were moving up and down Emma's back until she couldn't resist allowing them to slip down to rest on Emma's ass.

The sensation of Sophie's hands squeezing her ass, made her even hotter and she was barely in control of her hand as it moved out of Sophie's hair and onto her shoulder. Her fingers were lightly moving, caressing the bare skin of the neck, down to the shoulder and descending further down onto the girl's chest.

As Sophie felt this all she could think about was how much she wanted Emma to continue to move her hand down to grab and squeeze her tit. But something in her brain triggered and she remembered where they were, surrounded by people in the middle of a bar. Her eyes flew open as she checked around to see who was watching. Although it wasn't a gay bar, two girls kissing on the dance floor was hardly a rare occurrence so no one was really paying them much attention.

"Come on let's get out of here." Sophie said in a raised voice to be heard over the music.

"Right behind you" Emma followed up.

On the way out, they said a rushed goodbye to Tiffany. Emma pulled Sophie out of the bar and as soon as they were outside, she pushed her against the wall to continue their passionate kissing. She held her head and kissed all over Sophie's face from her forehead, down to her eyes, cheeks, chin and neck. As Sophie began to moan from the pleasure it was all she could do to open her eyes, grab Emma's arm and keep her moving towards the train station. Somewhere along the way they figured out that Emma's apartment was closest and as they couldn't wait to rip each other's clothes off, this seemed like the best option.

The train pulled up not long after they

arrived on the platform and unsurprisingly, considering the late hour, it was practically deserted. They found an empty carriage and Emma sat down, gesturing for Sophie to sit down next to her.

"Actually I think I'm gonna sit over here," and sat in the chair opposite.

Emma made a face, "How can I kiss you and touch you all the way over there?"

"Maybe I don't want you to kiss me and touch me... maybe I want you to look at me." As she said this Sophie slowly opened her legs, all the while keeping her eyes fixed on Emma's. She smiled as Emma broke the stare to glance down and look between the girl's legs. Sophie had been wearing a short skirt, which with her legs open now revealed some pink panties that was now sporting a wet spot. Sophie could feel her pussy getting wetter at the excitement of revealing herself like this, and she wouldn't have been surprised if her excitement was now visible to Emma.

"Do you see something you like?" Sophie asked playfully, whilst bringing her fingertips slowly up her legs from her knees and increasingly close to her pussy. When she reached the edges of her panties, she stopped for a moment but then continued and lightly brushed her slit from bottom to top one hand after another. She moaned lightly and then slipped her thumbs under her waistband, sliding them down slightly. "Should I carry on?"

Emma couldn't take her eyes off of the sight in front of her and was absentmindedly squeezing her own breasts and tugging at her nipples. On hearing the question, she swallowed. "Carry on."

The thrill of exposing herself was just as exciting to Sophie as it clearly was for Emma watching and spurred Sophie on. She slowly brought her underwear down, revealing her shaved pink cunt that was already glistening with her juices. She let her panties fall around her ankles where she kicked them off towards Emma and then let her hands return to playing around her inner thighs surrounding her pussy.

When Sophie's panties came flying towards her, Emma instinctively reached out to grab them. She brought them up to her face to smell Sophie's juices and the sweet aroma filled her nostril she felt a stream of wetness release from her own pussy. She closed her eyes and let out a soft moan.

Sophie wasn't expecting Emma to do that but seeing her smell her juices and the reaction she caused was too much for Sophie. Her pussy needed some direct stimulation so she brought her fingers to her hole and began making circles around her entrance. On seeing this, Emma could no longer stay still; she had smelt her juices but now she wanted a taste of Sophie's cunt. She stood up and knelt in front of the exposed blond girl. Holding Sophie's knees for support on the moving train, Emma began placing kisses on her inner thighs. She slowly moved up, getting closer and closer to her goal. She could see the pussy in front of her getting wetter in expectation and when she looked up she could see Sophie's face, watching and waiting, needing some attention on her throbbing clit. Part of Emma wanted to tease Sophie and make her wait, make her beg for it. But another side of her was desperate to have a taste of the juices that smelled so appealing.

As she continued kissing up her leg and reached the outer pussy, Emma switched her technique to light flicks of the tongue, rather than kisses. Then she used her hands to open Sophie, now fully exposing her wet hole and clitoris. She slowly licked all the way up one side before doing the same on the other side. All the time she was careful not to touch Sophie's clit; she wanted to make her wait for that. She circled her pussy hole a few times, gradually increasing the speed. She could feel the juices being released faster and thicker before finally using her tongue to penetrate Sophie's pussy as deep as she could.

At this Sophie's head fell backwards and she closed her eyes to fully enjoy the sensation of being fucked with another girl's tongue. Her moans was getting louder and more frequent as she remembered she was on a public train and attempted to stifle the noise with one hand. She felt Emma's tongue move up, beginning to approach her clit. She placed her other hand on Emma's head and attempted to direct her towards her clit. She couldn't wait anymore, she needed her clit to be stimulated and she wanted to cum.

When Emma felt Sophie's hand trying to direct her, she smiled to herself. She wanted to carry on teasing her but also wanted to make her cum. Finally, she approached Sophie's clit and began by slowly circling it. She picked up the pace and felt Sophie's hips gyrating along with her. She could feel her own pussy throbbing by this point and she also needed some attention. She reached one arm between her legs and unbuttoned her shorts. As she slid her hand inside and reached her own wet pussy, she let out an involuntary moan. Emma's moan created a sensual vibration against Sophie's clit, which caused her hips buck. She brought looked down and couldn't believe it was possible that she was turned on even more by the sight of Emma eating her out whilst masturbating herself.

Emma continued concentrating on Sophie's clit and sucked the whole thing into her mouth. Sophie almost let out a scream at this point and was past the point of caring who heard. She brought both hands to the back of Emma's head, keeping her face firmly in hcr pussy. Emma could hardly breathe but loved the effect she was causing. Sophie's hips and legs were now twitching and writhing uncontrollably and Emma had to hold them down to prevent them from squeezing her head too hard. She continued to suck in the hard nub, whilst licking the end of it as it was in her mouth. She knew how much Sophie was enjoying this and continued to do so. When she needed to take a second to breathe, she let go of her clit and gave a slow lick from the bottom of Sophie's slit all the way back up to the clit, wherc oncc again she took in into her mouth and sucked on in passionately. As she felt Sophie getting closer and closer to orgasm she removed her hand from her shorts, where she had been playing with herself and brought it up to the entrance of Sophie's hole. By this point Sophie was so wet that two fingers slid easily into her cunt and she slowly worked them in and out.

This had the desired effect and the whole of Sophie's body began to spasm. Her moaning got louder once again and now she was calling out to Emma.

"Oh yes, right there..."

"Don't stop...."

"Ahhh, I'm gonna cum!"

Emma had to fight with Sophie's writhing hips to keep her lips firmly around her clit but she managed to continue the stimulation, which finally brought Sophie over the edge. As she came down, Emma didn't let up and continued to finger fuck Sophie's pussy. As the sensitivity became too much on her clit she retreated to kissing the skin of her inner thighs once more but was determined to make Sophie come again, but this time with only her fingers. She continued to move them in and out and vary between this and massaging the inner walls of her pussy. She could feel the spongy wall of Sophie's G-spot and began to make circular motions over the area. Sophie who had calmed down to a soft humming noise began moaning loudly again, when she felt the pressure to her G-spot. Emma continued to work the area, building in speed and pressure until she was fairly roughly moving her hand in and out. She could feel the second orgasm building and knew that Sophie was close to exploding.

With a final scream, Sophie came and her juices flowed freely over Emma's hand. The girls looked at each other as they both attempted to catch their breath. Emma brought her hand up to taste her new friends cum before offering it to Sophie for a taste of her own juices. Sophie held Emma's wrist and slowly licked one of her fingers before taking it into her mouth and sensually sucking on it. The action reminded Emma of her own building tension and how much she also needed to cum.

Just as she was about to stand up, the train pulled to a stop. "Well this is my stop," Emma smiled. "I guess we better get off and continue this at my place."

"Damn right we're going to continue this at your place." Sophie went on, "Do you think I would let you go without a taste of your cum?"

The two girls shared a smile, straightened their clothes, got off the train and practically started running in the direction of Emma's apartment.

2 FUN IN THE SUN

I was sitting in one of my favorite little cafés located on the main high street of my town. Marie was due to join me for lunch and some girly chat. I really needed it today, as it had been two weeks since my split from Steve, and it was still really getting me down. I heard the soft ring of the bell that goes off every time the door of the café opens and turned my head to see if my friend had arrived. As I did so, I noticed a mirror on the wall to my left. I was close enough to see that I had bags under my eyes from a lack of sleep and too much crying. I resolved in that moment to get a hold of myself and to start taking care of my appearance again.

At 34, I'm reasonably happy with the

way I look. I have taken care of my body with a good diet and regular spinning sessions. My breasts are by far my favorite feature. Firm and perky D cups with gorgeous pink nipples that men tend to fall in love with at first sight. My hair, just like my eyes, is dark brown and falls just bellow my shoulders.

"Hey Julie," Marie called over. "How you doing?"

We sat in the café eating salad and drinking tea for a little over an hour. I told her all about my split with Steve and how hard I was taking it. We had only been together for about 6 months, but there had been talk of moving in together, and it really seemed to be heading in the right direction. He caught me completely off guard one afternoon by announcing that he was moving away and thought it was best to end the relationship. The bastard had even waited to get one last fuck out of me that morning before deciding to tell me.

"You know what you need? A holiday! Why don't you take a few days off work and get away for a while. Go somewhere sunny, lie on a beach, pamper yourself for a change and forget all about Steve."

"Like it's that easy," I laughed at Marie's suggestion.

"Why not? I think it would be good for you. It certainly couldn't hurt."

Marie's suggestion to take a break kept coming back to the forefront of my mind until finally I decided that it was a good idea and booked a cheap last-minute flight to Italy. I remembered that a friend last summer had recommended a great hotel that would even pick me up from the airport, so I wouldn't have to worry about anything. I packed my bag, but all the while I was wondering what the point was in all of this. I was sure that it wouldn't matter what country I was in, I was still going to miss Steve. In fact, the more I thought about it, the more absurd the idea seemed. Who goes on holiday by themselves? What am I going to do every day? Wander around an Italian city alone? More likely, I'll sit at the hotel bar and get drunk, I thought to myself as I zipped up my suitcase and headed out of the front door.

I arrived at my hotel, which was truly stunning. There were beautiful white bungalow-style villas dotted around amongst palm trees and sandy paths. The sun was shining, giving my body natural warmth that I hadn't felt for a long time, and I could see just past the villas the vast area of white sand and blue sea. As I was shown to my villa, I noticed a swimming pool and bar and made a mental note to myself that that would be my first port of call.

The room was simple, clean and white with an enormous bed in the middle and an en suite bathroom. I dumped my suitcase, quickly put my bikini on and grabbed a towel. I couldn't wait to enjoy the feel of the sunshine on my skin as I laid next to the pool with a cocktail and a book.

As it was low season, there were plenty of loungers available and even better... no kids. I laid my towel on one of the sun loungers and headed over to the bar. I was comfortable enough with my body to walk around in only a bikini, especially as there were a couple of other women doing the same thing, and I was fairly confident that I had the best body. My bikini was white with simple bottoms and a top that left little to the imagination. The cups covered my nipples and not a lot more so there was plenty of cleavage on show.

I approached the bar and for the first time noticed the bartender. He was shirtless and obviously Italian, with gorgeous smooth tanned skin and a body that he was clearly proud of. His abs were incredibly defined, and I found myself wondering if this was the most ribbed body I had ever seen in real life! His hair was jet black and his eyes had a piercing sparkle to them. A smile appeared across his face, and he had obviously noticed that I had been checking him out. I had not been subtle at all. I felt my cheeks warming up as I blushed slightly and quickly ordered a drink and rushed back to my spot. I had a lovely and relaxing afternoon lying by the pool, drinking numerous cocktails, and had become so enthralled by my book that I hardly noticed that the sun was beginning to set. I looked around the pool and realized that everyone was gone. I took the opportunity to have the pool to myself and dove straight in to the deep end. As I got out, I saw the bartender coming towards me.

"Sorry to disturb you, I just wanted to let you know that I am closing the pool bar soon, so if you would like another drink, you should order now."

His voice was deep with a strong accent that meant I had to concentrate hard on what he was saying. I was watching his lips to help me recognize the words, and when he finished, I looked back up to his eyes. I couldn't help but smile as I realized he couldn't take his eyes off my breasts. I looked down and saw that the water had made my bikini practically see-through. My nipples were hard from the cool air and poking through the sheer material.

"Do you see something you like?" I surprised myself when I heard my own voice. I wasn't sure if it was the cocktails, the foreign country, or my recent heartbreak that had made me so forward. He looked up when he heard me speak and looked into my eyes with that sparkle. He took a step forward and reached for my hand. He brought it into his crotch for me to feel his semi-hard cock. He held my wrist and guided my hand up and down his shaft and I could feel it growing underneath my fingers. He bit his bottom lip and let out a slight whimper.

Everything about the situation was turning me on: the fact that we stood in an open public area, the fact that I was wet and almost naked, the feel of the soft cool breeze against my erect nipples, and of course, the hard cock that I could feel throbbing in my hand. I now had a firm grip of his penis through his shorts. The bartender, whose name I did not yet know, was still guiding my hand and beginning to increase the pace. Our bodies were quite close together now, and every so often, my nipples would graze against his chest. Every time it happened, we both felt a little jolt and I could feel my pussy getting wetter and wetter.

I could feel his chest moving up and down as his breathing became deeper. His hips were moving in circles as he varied the pressure of my hand on his cock. All the time I kept a good grip and let him masturbate himself with my hand. He kept increasing the speed, and his breathing was getting faster and faster. Finally, he pushed his body in close to me and kissed hard the side of my neck. He let out a long moan, and I felt his body spasm slightly. He stopped moving my hand but kept it on him, keeping his cock firmly between my hand and his body.

It took a few seconds for his breathing to return to normal, but once it did, he whispered into my ear. "I'm Paolo, come to villa 12 at 7 o'clock." With that, he turned and walked away.

The time seemed to drag on forever before it was finally 7 p.m. During that time, I had taken a shower to get the chlorine off my skin but also in attempt to cool myself down. Ever since the incident at the pool, I hadn't been able to think about anything else, and as a result, I had been getting progressively more turned on and my pussy was throbbing with the need for attention. I had considered a number of times in the last hour or so whether to go through with it and actually thought what the hell I was thinking. These thoughts, however, were always replaced with the memory of his cock in my hand and the warmth of his smooth, firm body against my chest. At 7 o'clock, I took a deep breath and left my room for villa 12. I had been worrying constantly about what to wear and had finally landed on a patterned blue maxi dress. It hugged my figure and showed off my breasts, and I was pretty certain that we wouldn't be wearing clothes for long anyway.

It turned out that I was right. Paolo opened the door with just a small towel around his waist. I instinctively looked around to check that nobody else was around as he ushered me inside. I was suddenly feeling very shy and self-conscious. Any effects for the afternoon's alcohol intake had clearly worn off, and I now felt very awkward and had no idea what to do. Paolo, however, was clearly not having the same problem. He closed the door behind him and immediately removed the towel to reveal his erection. I couldn't resist letting my gaze wander and take a look at the cock that I had not yet seen but had already jerked off. It was beautiful. Not the biggest I had ever seen at around 7 inches, but it was thick with a smooth head that I already knew I wanted to lick.

He walked towards me slowly and, as he reached me, took my head in both of his hands and brought his lips to mine. He gave me a deep and sensual kiss that instantly made me relax. As we kissed, his hands moved slowly down the back of my head and found the strings that were holding my dress up. He pulled one side, and I felt the dress loosen as he let it fall down my body into a heap around my feet. As soon as the dress had fallen, his hands returned to my back searching for my bra clasp. He had it undone in moments without me even realizing. He broke the kiss and moved away from my body so that he could seductively take my bra strap down each arm and off completely. The whole time, he had been looking me in the eye, but in this moment, he took the opportunity to look down and take in the sight of my bare chest. He bent his head and took my left nipple into his mouth, sucking on it and lightly grazing his teeth against it. The sudden sensation felt amazing, and I couldn't suppress a moan. He switched breasts and took the other nipple in his mouth and looked up into my eyes.

I was moaning softly, enjoying the feeling, and my eyes were beginning to close. All of a sudden, Paolo picked me up and carried me over to the bed. He laid me down and was on top of me, kissing all over my face and working down my neck. I could feel his cock poking into my stomach, and as he kissed me, I could feel him moving ever so slightly up and down, enjoying the pressure it created. He moved further and further down my body, and I knew he was making his way down to taste my wet pussy. I grabbed his shoulders to indicate that I didn't want him to go any further. He looked up at me, "What's wrong?"

"Stop," I said. "I want your cock in my mouth."

He smiled and started moving back up my body. He gave me one last passionate kiss on the lips and then pulled himself up onto his knees straddling my face. I took in the sight of his smooth cock and balls so close to my face and then brought one hand up to guide the head of his penis into my mouth. I gave it a light lick, tasting his pre-cum before sucking the entire head into my mouth. He was so thick that I only just fit it into my mouth, and the thought of it filling my pussy was making me crazy. He slowly pushed his hips forward to get more of his cock in my mouth, and I continued to suck and flick my tongue across the head. I took my other hand up to fondle his balls, causing his eyes to close and his head to drop back. I was slowly moving my head back and forwards in time with his hips so Paolo was now fucking my mouth.

Paolo took his hand behind him and found my wet hole. He slowly rubbed up and down my slit, and feeling how wet I was, he quickly put two fingers inside my pussy and started to fuck me with them. Getting the attention that I so desperately needed had me moaning instantly, and

Paolo clearly loved the feeling of the vibrations from my mouth on his cock.

"Ahhh yeah, you like that don't you? You like me finger fucking your pussy don't you?"

"Hmmm," was the only sound I could make with his cock filling my mouth.

"I bet you want my fat cock in your pussy don't you?"

All I could do was look at him and nod my head. With that, he pulled out of my mouth and moved down to put the head of his cock against the entrance of my wet pussy. He slowly rubbed his cock up and down my cunt a few times before finally plunging it all the way into me. I let out a loud scream as he completely filled my slick pussy.

He began thrusting hard immediately as neither of us could take much more. We were both so excited that all we wanted to do was cum. He pumped in and out of me and I matched him with my hips. I had been waiting since the pool for some release, and I knew if he carried on like this, it wouldn't be long before I got there. Both of our breathing had become labored, and we were moaning almost simultaneously. My nails scratched into his back as I tried to pull him closer to get his cock as deep into my cunt as possible. My hips were bouncing up and down on the bed, and I was kissing his neck to keep him close to me. Finally, Paolo sped up one final time, and our moans became louder and louder until eventually, we both came at the same time. He collapsed on top of me and that's where he stayed, until we had recovered enough to go again.

3 SHOPPING SENSATIONS

I was bored one weekend with no work to worry about and no plans with friends, so I decided to head off to the shopping mall. It was a particularly hot day so I was looking forward to the air conditioning more than actually shopping. I was pretty casual wearing a simple pair of shorts and one of those baggy tops that stop just before your belly button with a tie, kind of cowboy style. I'm 23 and while I know my body is nowhere near as good as some of the girls I see, I'm pretty happy with it. My stomach is relatively flat and I have nicely toned legs. If I could change one thing I would probably make my tits bigger. I'm just about a 32 B, easily the smallest out of my group of best friends, which sometimes makes me feel self-conscious. Sometimes, when we're at the gym or going swimming I can't help but have a look at their naked bodies. I'm not a lesbian or anything; I think I just like to look because they are so different from mine.

So anyway, I was walking around the mall, kind of browsing and going into shops here and there if something in the window caught my eye. I was just thinking about going to get some lunch when I saw a cute pink top on display. I walked into the shop and began to look around, hoping to see where they had the top stocked.

Once I was in there, I realized that there were a number of items I liked so I grabbed a few things and thought I would try some of them on. I walked over to the dressing room and there was a shop assistant counting how many items each person had and asking if they needed any help. She took my items to count them and I couldn't help but stare at her chest. She was wearing a button up shirt, which was the uniform for the store, but she had left a couple of buttons at the top undone. I could clearly see her cleavage and her boobs filled out that shirt very nicely. She went to hand me back my items, but as she did so, she brought them back towards her body so that her hand was just above her chest. As she did this, I naturally grabbed for the hangers but ended up grazing the side of one of her tits. She laughed and I grabbed my items, walked to the furthest free changing room, a little embarrassed and annoyed that she had laughed at me.

I got into my changing room, then shut and locked the door. I realized that I was flustered but wasn't sure why. Was it because I had stared at her tits? Had she seen and purposely moved the clothes towards her so I would touch her? Or was I flustered because I had looked at her tits and wanted to touch them? I took a deep breath and sat down on the stool in the corner of the room.

"Stop overreacting," I told myself. "She didn't see you look, you touched her boob by accident, she isn't thinking anything more about it and neither should you." With that, I shook it off and started trying on the clothes I had picked up.

There was a black halter-top that I liked but it was a little too big. I really wanted to try a smaller size on but that would mean talking to the girl again. I took the top off and stuck my head outside the door.

"Excuse me? Could I try this one in a smaller size please?"

The girl left her station, smiled at me, and started walking over. All I could think was "Don't look at her tits, don't look at her tits." Therefore, I was basically staring at her in the eyes the entire time that she walking towards me, and she also didn't break eye contact. When she was close enough, I could see her eyes were a greenish brown color. Her hair was blonde and other than her breasts, her body was pretty small. She was right outside my room now taking the shirt from me and I realized how beautiful her face was. Her skin was flawless and her lips were full and pink with some shiny lip-gloss. Oh god, was I staring at her lips now? She took the shirt and I uttered a "thank you." "What's wrong with me?" I thought as the girl walked back out of the dressing room and into the main store to find my shirt. "I'm probably freaking her out; she's going to think I'm gay."

She came back a couple of minutes later with the shirt in a smaller size. "Why don't you let me help you?" she suggested. "These shirts can be difficult to tie up by yourself."

I didn't respond for a moment. I currently had just my head and one arm out the door because I was only wearing my bra and my shorts. I didn't know how to respond, as I didn't really feel comfortable with a stranger seeing me without a top. "Come on, it's my job. You don't have to be shy!"

So I let her in the room. She handed me the shirt and then turned around to lock the door. I turned around to face the wall so that I would have my back to her. I put the shirt on and then I felt her hands on my back as she reached to tie the shirt. It gave me a bit of a shock and I jolted away from her. She laughed again, in the same way as before, and then pulled me back and continued to tie the shirt. Finally, she placed her hands on my hips and turned me around to face her. "Hey, that looks great." As she said it her hands were on my stomach, smoothing down the material and then they moved up and rubbed over my small mounds. I moved back a little and she knew I was uncomfortable. She looked me in the eye, "It's only fair," she said. "You got a feel of mine."

"That was an accident," I replied, a little too fast and forceful.

"Come on, I saw you looking. You wanted a feel!"

"What! I...I... was looking at your name badge."

"Oh really!" The girl said with a smirk and used her hand to cover her badge. "So what's my name?"

"Fuck!" I thought. I had vaguely noticed the name badge but certainly not thoroughly enough to take in her name. Of course, this was because she was right, I had been looking at her tits, but I couldn't admit that.

"Do you want a better look?" she asked. Before I could say a word, she was unbuttoning her shirt. She got to the last one and then threw her shirt on the floor. She was still looking at me with that cheeky grin and I was trying my best to hold eye contact with her. I couldn't stop myself from glancing down for the briefest of moments but she saw and laughed again.

"My name's Leah by the way, and now it's your turn."

"My name's Rachel," I replied.

"Hi Rachel, but I meant now it's your turn to take your top off."

"No way, you're crazy." I started gathering my belongings.

Leah laughed again. "Just relax will you. I know you want this. Look!"

She took off her bra and left it in a pile with her shirt. I stopped what I was doing, mainly because I was shocked at how confident and forward this girl was being, but also because her bare breasts were a sight that I couldn't turn away from. Not only did I want to look but also I wanted to touch, and she knew it. She took both of my hands in hers and gently placed them on her tits. Then, she took a step forward and lightly kissed my bottom lip. She moved up slightly to kiss me full and passionately on the lips. Her tongue darted into my mouth and I sucked on another girl's tongue for the first time. It was so sensual and soft. I never would have imagined that kissing a girl would be so different from kissing a guy; the softness of her lips, the sweet smell of her skin, and the feel of her breasts in my hands. All of a sudden, I felt hot. This girl was turning me on, and I could feel it all over my body. My hairs were standing up, my legs felt weak, and my pussy was getting wetter and wetter. I was sure that she was having a similar reaction as the kiss became more passionate and more forceful.

My hands were still cupping her tits but by now my inhibitions were disappearing and I started to squeeze them and rub my fingers in little circles over her nipples. She was letting out little moans into my mouth, which only spurred me on. Her hands began to explore my body, too. She pushed them under my shirt and like an expert undid my bra clasp. She broke the kiss only for a second to pull off my shirt and bra. As soon as they were off our lips locked again. She spent some time massaging my tits and tugging on my nipples, which I have never enjoyed so much in my life.

Finally, her hands began to work their way down and she undid my shorts button and zipper. She tried to push them down over my ass and I had to help a bit by wriggling out of them. By this point, I wasn't shy at all. I was having too much fun and I knew that I had good legs. At this point, Leah broke away from my lips. She began to kiss down my neck and I reciprocated until she was too low down and I could no longer reach. When she took almost my entire breast into her mouth, I let out an involuntary gasp. She sucked on it and flicked her tongue over my nipple. The sensations were incredible. It was as though little electric shocks were travelling from my nipple to my pussy, which was beginning to throb with excitement and expectation.

I was a little disappointed when she had finished working my tits and began to place soft kisses on my stomach. But this too felt amazing and I couldn't believe how exciting it was to see a beautiful girl's head making her way towards my pussy. By this point, I could feel the juices running out of my cunt and I couldn't wait for her to reach my hole and start to lap them up.

Leah could see how excited she was making me but was taking her time to get to her destination. Every time I let out a moan, she would look up at me with that smile and her eyes would glisten revealing that she was just as excited as I was. She reached the edge of my panties and slowly brought them down my legs, and as she did so she indicated for me to take a seat on the little corner chair. I sat on the edge with my legs spread and watched as the beautiful blonde kissed the inside of my knee and made her way up my inner thigh. I was sure that she must have been able to smell my excitement. Just as I thought, she was about to reach my cunt, she pulled away and placed a kiss on the inner knee of my other leg. I almost grunted with frustration and I could see in her eyes that Leah knew exactly what she was doing to me. This time as she approached my pussy, I put my hands on the back of her head so that she couldn't get away.

She looked up at me one last time and then just like that she was sucking my clit into her mouth between her teeth. My hand flew up to my mouth to stifle a scream.

"Ahhhhh! Oh my god!"

I had never experienced such intense pleasure. She kept my clit in her mouth while at the same time flicking her tongue over it and stimulating it with little circular movements. Occasionally, when she knew I was getting close, she would let it go and give long slow licks all the way from my ass hole back up to my clit. Just as I was calming down, she would suck my clit back in again and work me back up to the edge over and over again. I don't know how many times she did this before finally I couldn't take any more. I put my hands firmly on the back of her head as my hips began to gyrate uncontrollably. Leah managed to keep her mouth firmly over my clit and continued to lick and suck until my body had relaxed again.

"Oh my god, that was amazing." I slid off the chair to join her on the floor. I hugged her tightly and we began to kiss again. "It's your turn," I whispered into her ear and I felt her shiver. I pushed her down so that she was lying on her back with her knees bent. There was only just enough room to do this in the small changing room. I licked all the way from her ear to left nipple and then I danced around it with my tongue. As I was playing with her tits, I let my hand wander down to her pussy. As I reached her slit, I couldn't believe how wet she was. "Wow," I whispered. "You're so wet."

"That's because you make me so hot... I want you to fuck me."

"Oh yeah? You want me to fuck you with my fingers or my tongue?"

"Mmmm," she moaned from a combination of me lightly biting her nipple and from hearing me talk about fucking her.

"I want both."

I gave her tits a final kiss and then moved between her legs. I could smell her juices and I couldn't wait to taste my first girl. I put my hands on her thighs and pushed them both back and out, opening her up more to me. I saw her cunt open, and I could see the juices coating her inner lips. I slowly leaned in to lightly lick her pussy. Then, I began to lick in circles around her hole and I could feel her juices coming out faster and faster and I couldn't get enough. I wanted to lick it all up. I looked up to see that Leah had put her top over her face in an attempt to stifle some of her moans.

Seeing this made me want to get her to moan louder and uncontrollably. I moved my tongue up to locate her clit and began to tease her by licking around it. I avoided touching it until Leah began to use her hips to try and guide me to give it some attention. Finally, I did so and at the same time, I gently inserted two fingers inside her cunt. I began to slowly move them in and out while simultaneously massaging her g-spot with my fingertips. This caused the reaction I was hoping for and Leah's moans were getting louder and louder. Her body was beginning to squirm and her hips would not stay on the floor. I tried my best to keep doing everything I was doing despite her frantic movements.

"I'm gonna cum! Don't stop!"

There was no way I was going to stop. I loved the reaction I was causing this beautiful girl. I kept going until I felt a stream of juices running from her cunt at which point I took out my fingers and began to lick it up. I couldn't believe how much I enjoyed licking a girl's pussy and making her cum.

We both took a few minutes to calm down and agreed that I should try to make it into the store for as many of Leah's shifts as possible.

4 A BANGING BIRTHDAY

One weekend last summer, I was around Jess' house. We were talking about our mutual friend Mark, and how it was his birthday coming up the following week. We all knew each other from university as we shared a couple of the same classes. Jess and I hit it off fairly quickly and started hanging out most of the time. We saw Mark sitting alone one day, eating lunch in the cafeteria, and asked him to join us. After that day, the three of us pretty much ate lunch together every day.

Now two years later, the friendship was still going strong. Jess started seeing some guy a few months ago though, and we had been seeing less and less of her. Fortunately, he had gone away with his family for the summer, so he wasn't coming to Mark's the following week. Neither Mark nor I had really taken to him and Jess was aware of that. I think that's partly why we were both so excited as we sat in Jess' room discussing the party and trying to decide what to wear. Jess was trying on this simple black dress. It was short and strapless with some details over the chest and exposed a lot of flesh. I couldn't help but admire her body in that outfit. Jess is curvy with the best ass I've ever seen and toned legs that were being displayed perfectly in that dress. There was also a decent amount of cleavage visible, so all in all, I didn't know where to look! Jess noticed this and laughed.

"Hello, earth to Holly!"

"Huh?" I said, finally looking up and into her deep blue eyes.

"I asked you what you think of this one!"

"Oh sorry. It looks great. You should definitely wear this one next week; I think Mark might have a heart attack." I stood up and started squeezing Jess' boobs with both hands. This was normal behavior for us and I didn't think anything of it. She knew I was jealous of her big tits, as mine were barely a handful; more like little mounds. Every so often I would have a play and we have been known to kiss occasionally too, but that was usually only after a drink or two.

"Well at least that's something to give him. I haven't gotten him a gift yet. Have you?"

"Nope. I was thinking we could get him something from both of us. Might be a bit cheaper that way. He won't mind. He knows we're both broke! You got any ideas?"

"Actually you're kind of giving me an idea right now." Jess looked down at my hands on her breasts and raised an eyebrow.

"Give him your tits?" I joked. "Come on. I have first dibs on these."

"No, I was thinking we could give him a bit of a show. Nothing crazy. Just let him watch us kiss. It's no big deal for us, but he would love it. Let's be honest. What 20-year-old wouldn't?"

I thought about it and couldn't stop a little smile creeping across my face. It sounded like a great idea. It was always fun when Jess and I had our little make-out sessions, and it would be even more fun seeing Mark enjoy it. He had jokingly requested for us to kiss when we had been out drinking together, but Jess and I had always wanted to be in private before having any fun. We were both into guys and didn't want to spark any rumors around the campus that weren't true.

"I'm in!"

The next week I found myself thinking about Mark's party on a regular basis. I couldn't wait to see his reaction and I can't deny that the idea of the situation was turning me on. Jess and I had planned out the whole thing. Mark was having his party on the Friday night, but we decided that we would go earlier to help him set up. We would give him his "present" then, before the rest of his friends turned up. I couldn't wait for the day to arrive.

Friday afternoon, a couple of hours before the party was supposed to start, I went by Jess' to pick her up and then we made our way to Mark's house. We were already in our party outfits so Jess was wearing that stunning black dress. I watched her as she walked down her drive. Now she was wearing heels as well, which just accentuated her legs, making them even sexier. She had curled her long brown hair, and as she walked, she flicked it out of her eyes. She came closer and gave me a big smile and a hug.

"Excited?" she asked me.

"Sure am!"

We got to Mark's house and knocked on the door. We could already hear music playing from the inside, and all of a sudden, the door flung open. Mark was wearing a pair of shorts and tee shirt—clearly not yet dressed for the party. Mark was a very handsome 20-year-old with dark hair and eyes. He hadn't had much experience with girls, and although he was bubbly and confident around his close friends, many people considered him to be shy.

"Wow, you two look amazing!" He gave us both a quick squeeze and then ushered us inside the house. We spent about an hour sorting out the front room, making space for dancing and an area in the kitchen for bottles of alcohol, mixers, and ice buckets. Mark had already bought quite a few bottles, but no doubt the party guests would bring more. Not long after arriving, we had opened the first bottle of vodka and were now on our second glasses of vodka coke. As the house was just about ready, we all sat down. Jess and I sat on one sofa and Mark on the adjacent one. Jess caught my eye and raised her eyebrow. I nodded my head and smiled.

"Mark... Holly and I have got you a joint present this year," Jess was smiling and her eyes were twinkling.

"Aw, you didn't have to, you guys. I'm just happy to have you here. And thanks for your help today by the way. Where is it then? You didn't bring anything in with you!"

"Well, it's more what we're going to do rather than what we're going to give you."

"Riiight," Mark's face was suddenly both confused and intrigued.

Jess stood up, came, and walked in front of me on the sofa. I was about to stand up to join her when all of a sudden she put one leg over me and straddled me, sitting on my lap. Doing this with such a short dress meant that it rode up nearly all of the way to her hips so the entire lengths of her legs were exposed to me. I was a little taken aback as we hadn't discussed this. I presumed that we would just stand up in front of Mark and kiss. I glanced over at Mark, who was staring in disbelief. Jess was looking at me dead in the eye and smiling, seemingly happy to have shocked both Mark and me. I put my hands on her thighs and began to slowly move them up and down. She had her hands on my side.

Jess began to lean her head down towards me as she came in to kiss me. Our lips met very softly, barely touching at first but slowly becoming firmer. Both of our eyes closed and I felt Jess' tongue gently parting my lips. My lips were almost tingling with the sensation of her tongue penetrating my mouth, and I met her with my own tongue. She tasted sweet, like the vodka coke we had been drinking. As the kiss continued, our tongues became more forceful and I sucked Jess' into my mouth. As I did this, she let out a soft moan, which allowed me to know that she was enjoying it. It wasn't only for show.

We continued like this for a good few minutes. Occasionally I would open my eyes to glance over and see what Mark was doing. As he was only wearing shorts, I could easily see that there was now a tent shape emerging in the front. I was secretly quite impressed at how big it looked. The sensations of the passionate kiss with my best friend and the sight of the reaction it was causing on Mark were incredibly stimulating. All of a sudden, I could feel my pussy aching and knew that I was already wet. I was sure that Jess was having a similar reaction as she was now very subtly grinding on my lap.

I couldn't stop my hands from wandering from Jess' incredibly smooth and silky legs, over her dress up her stomach, to her wonderful boobs. As soon as I got there, I could feel that she wasn't wearing a bra under the dress, and as I squeezed her tits, I found her hard nipples. I pinched and tugged at them both at the same time, eliciting another moan from her. This one was loud enough for Mark to hear and triggered him to free his cock from his shorts. Now I saw Mark's cock for the first time. It was long but not too fat and curled slightly to the left. It was already rock-hard as Mark slowly began to jerk his rod.

I wanted Jess to get a look at the beautiful sight of Mark's cock in his hand, but I knew that she wouldn't be able to while kissing me. I didn't want to break the kiss in case it meant the end of Mark's "present," but I was fairly sure that everyone involved was enjoying it far too much to stop. I decided that the best thing to do was to move the kiss down Jess' neck so that we haven't really stopped and she would be able to turn her head to look over to Mark. I took my tongue from Jess' mouth and licked all the way from her mouth, down her neck, to her chest. Here I began placing wet kisses all over the tops of her boobs that were exposed in the dress. At first, she just watched me covering her chest with little licks and kisses. Then she seemed to remember Mark sitting behind her and turned around. I felt that she took a deep breath in as she got her first sight. By now, Mark had his shorts around his ankles and top up to his chest and was stroking his cock with one hand while fondling his balls with the other. She looked back at me and smiled; then she reached for my chin and brought my head up. I thought she was going to kiss me again, but she went past my lips and whispered something to my ear.

"Let's ask him to join in."

I could hear the excitement in her voice and knew she was enjoying this as much as I was. She climbed off me and gestured for Mark to come over and take over in her position. He stood up, properly removed his shorts and tee shirt, then walked over, and got on top of me without skipping a beat. He immediately kissed my lips firmly and passionately. Jess sat down beside us and reached between our bodies, grabbing Mark's cock. As soon as she took hold of it, Mark pushed down, making our kiss even deeper.

Jess held his cock firmly and began to move her hand up and down. Every time she brought her fingertips over the head, I could feel him breathe in and his stomach tense. With one hand on him, she brought her free one up to my dress and let my straps fall over my shoulder. This gave her some accessibility to my tits, and she immediately began tugging on my nipples, alternating between them.

When Mark realized my nipples were out, he bent his head, flicked his tongue over them, and sucked them in hard. I was moaning constantly at this point and was starting to crave some attention to my pussy. I looked over at Jess to see her stand up and let her dress fall. She returned to the sofa, with her back against the far arm and her feet up close to us. She pulled her panties to the side, exposing her wet cunt to me, and immediately inserted two fingers into her pussy. The sight was too much for me and I felt as though a soft breeze across my pussy would be enough to make me cum. Mark was still enjoying the taste of my nipples so I bent my head down to whisper in his ear.

"I want you to fuck me."

That was all the encouragement he needed to stand up and drag me to the edge of the sofa. He pushed both my knees and dress up to my stomach and, with one hand, pulled my underwear down my legs and off. In this position, both my pussy and asshole were completely exposed to him. Holding my legs in place, he bent his head and took a lick of my pussy. He delved his tongue deep into my hole, tasting my juices that were already pouring out of me by this point. He spent a couple of minutes fucking me with his tongue before I pulled his head up. I needed his cock. I needed to be fucked.

He stood up and positioned his cock at the entrance of my pussy. He lent forward and, with one thrust, had penetrated deep into my pussy. I screamed out with such pleasure as he began to fuck me, filling me with every thrust. All of a sudden, there was some movement next to us, and Jess was standing on the couch and putting one leg over me so that she was now straddling my face and lowering her pussy to my mouth. "Oh my god," I thought. I'm about to eat another girl's pussy. As she lowered her cunt to me, I opened my mouth slightly and stuck out my tongue. I flicked my tongue over her clit and then moved down to taste the juices from her hole.

I couldn't believe how sweet she was. And I loved how she moaned and reacted when I did certain things. Occasionally I would go back to her clit and suck it into my mouth. Every time I did it, she would start to grind in circular motions on my face. The taste and smell of Jess' pussy, not to mention the feeling of Mark's cock fucking me, meant that it would not be long before I was going to cum. As I began to moan harder from the intense pleasure, the vibrations from my mouth on Jess' clit were bringing her to the edge. The sight of Jess sitting on my face and me lapping up her juices with such enthusiasm was becoming too much for Mark, and he was fucking me harder and harder, now desperate for his release.

All three of us were moaning and screaming and getting closer and closer until finally I felt Jess' cum streaming out from her pussy and into my mouth. This was all it took me and my pussy began to contract around Mark's cock as my orgasm shook through me. The tightening of my muscles around his throbbing cock milked the cum out of him, and he pulled out just in time to cum all over my pussy and thighs.

The three of us were in a mixture of shock and post-orgasm recovery when the doorbell rang. "Fuck, the party," Mark said, jumping up. He turned back and smiled at us before running up to the stairs to get changed. I turned to look at Jess. We both laughed out loud, as we considered what we just did, and before cleaning up and answering the door, we vowed to give Mark the same present next year.

5 OVERTIME

I am a partner at a law firm, and as much as I love my job, the thing that I really enjoy is being the boss. I have a number of employees who work on my floor, and whilst I think I am a fair and friendly boss, I do like to abuse my power every now and then. I know I have a reputation amongst some of my staff as being scary, and I find it kind of funny that people think that about me. I sometimes tell friends from outside of work what people have said about me, and they can't believe it.

I'm 35, which is quite young to have already made partner. I think that's partly what people find intimidating about me as I'm intelligent and have a very strong work ethic. I can't stand slackers, and everyone knows they have to pull their weight if they are going to work for me. I'm not bad looking either, if I do say so myself. I have always taken care of myself. I go to the gym regularly and take pride in my appearance. A typical outfit for the office may be a pencil skirt with a fitted shirt and heels. I always wear high heels because I love the way it makes my calves look sexy and toned. I'm aware of the looks that I get from both men and women when I'm walking around, and it turns me on when I know I'm being checked out.

One morning, there was a light tap at my office door. "Come in!"

The door opened slowly and on the other side stood Luke. He has been working for me for about 6 months now, and I am pleased with the work he has so far produced. Aside from being a good worker, he also looks great. He always dresses very smartly often with a full suit and tie and is obviously a hard worker. Some evenings he would stay behind late and take the liberty to remove his shirt jacket and tie. The couple of times that I have seen this, I couldn't help but notice his chest and arm muscles were very defined, and I secretly relished the chance to get a better look and preferably a good feel.

He walked inside and flashed me a smile. He had a cute smile that revealed little cheek dimples that even a stern woman such as myself couldn't help but adore. Normally, when people came to find me in my office, it was because they needed a signature or wanted to go over some document or other with me. On this occasion, however, I noticed that Luke did not have anything in his hands.

"How can I help you Luke?" I asked without taking my eyes away from the papers on my desk.

"Actually, I wanted to ask a favor from you."

This caught my attention for as I said earlier, it's not often that one of my employers would dare ask me for something. I looked up from the computer screen to see Luke nervously touching the back of his head. "And what might that be?"

"Well, the thing is my sister is coming into town.... And well, I was wondering if I could have tomorrow and Friday off to show her around."

"Hmm." Nothing irritated me more than people wanting time off at the last minute. "And what about the Johnson case, I suppose you have everything ready for that?"

"Yes, nearly everything. Lisa is wrapping up the last few details, and I still have time on Monday to go over everything once more with the client."

"Right. Well, I see you've thought things through. So if I were to say no, what would your sister do then?"

"Well, I guess she would have to stay at my place or walk around town by herself. Either way, I don't think she would have much of a good time."

"Hmm. I'll think about it. Come back later, and I'll let you know by the end of the day."

I already knew that I was going to let him go. He had finished his work, and I wasn't so heartless that I would expect him to neglect his family. But even so, I didn't want to look like a pushover, I had a reputation to maintain and if I make it easy for one, they would all be asking. I didn't want Luke thinking that his charming smile and attitude was working on me either; there's nothing worse than a lawyer with a big ego. I wanted to think of a way to show him that even though I was giving him time off, I was still his boss. I spent the rest of the afternoon with different ideas going round my mind until finally I thought of something that would not only remind him who's in charge but would also make my day a little more fun.

It was well after 6 before I noticed a shadow lurking outside my office door and Luke's gentle knock once again.

"Come in."

"Hi Linda, I was wondering if you...."

"Close the door behind you," I cut him off. I knew by this time most people would have left to go home and the few that remained wouldn't bother me at this time of day.

Luke looked a little surprised at being interrupted but took a few steps forward and closed the door behind him.

"Lock it."

At the sound of this instruction, Luke looked up and stared me right in the eye, as if asking me what I was up to. I could see something come alive in his eyes, but his expression didn't change, and he didn't say a word. He simply turned slowly, pushed the button in to lock the door and then turned back to look at me. I knew already from the look in his eyes that he was going to do anything I asked of him.

"Remove your jacket and tie."

Luke did so, the whole time maintaining eye contact with me. Then he took a couple of steps towards my desk and gently placed his jacket over the back of the chair opposite mine. I remained coolly sat in my chair, but I could feel my heart rate beginning to quicken at the thought of how far this might go. His hand went up to the top of his shirt, undid the top button, and then came back to his sides.

"Don't stop."

"Don't stop what." He said in a voice that sounded deeper than usual which lead me to suspect that he had to force it to prevent it from breaking.

"The buttons. Undo them all."

He looked at me now with a slight smirk on his face as if to say, "Are you serious? Are we really doing this?" After a few moments of eye contact, I raised my eyebrows, so he would know that I was serious. Finally, he brought both hands up and began to unbutton his shirt one by one. I tried to disguise it but may not have done a very good job when a small smile came over my face. His body was perfect, much better than I had previously thought. His muscles were toned just the way I like it. Not bodybuilder big, which I find horrible but with just enough definition to be truly sexy. My favorite part on any man is those two lines that go from either side of the abdomen down to the groin. Whenever I saw that on a man, I find it hard to suppress the desire to leave long kisses all the way down it.

He took his shirt off and left it on the chair with his jacket. He just stood there looking at me waiting for the next instructions. "Come over here," I said.

He walked over to me where I was sitting behind my desk. I waited until he was right in front of me before reaching up and undoing his belt buckle. I pulled his belt all the way off and threw it on the floor. Then I came back to undo his top button and fly and let his trousers drop around his ankles. Now my face was just a few inches from his tight white boxers and the clear outline of his growing hard-on. I think subconsciously I may have licked my lips. I reached around to feel his firm ass cheeks, and I looked at him in the eye as I dragged my manicured nails across his cheeks. I brought them all the way around from his ass back round over the top of his thighs until my fingertips met the base of his cock. Through his boxers, I gently dragged my fingertips from either side of the base all the way down to the head. I could feel him getting harder as I did so.

I was enjoying the feel of his cock, but I wanted to see it. I slipped my fingers into the edge of his boxers and slowly pulled them down, allowing his now fully erect cock to spring free. It was a nice size at about 7 inches long with a nice fat girth. I love a cock that could fill me up and this would certainly do the job.

I told him to take step back so that I could take in his entire glorious body. He did so, stepping out of his trousers and boxers at the same time. I looked his body up and down and was shocked at how erotic I found it to be looking at a naked man whilst I was still fully dressed. I could feel my pussy beginning to get slick from my juices and was debating in my head what action I should take next.

I hitched my skirt up slightly and then removed my tights, leaving them in a ball on the floor. I opened my legs directing them towards Luke and knew that my underwear would be exposed to him in this position. I began to rub my slit over my panties and couldn't help but bite my bottom lip as I enjoyed the attention to my pussy.

"Do you like this?" I asked Luke. "Do you like the sight of me pleasuring myself?"

"Yes," he said with a dry voice and then immediately swallowed. I could see some pre-cum beginning to seep out the tip of his penis.

"Why don't you come over here and help me..."

Luke took a few steps forwards towards my chair. I gestured for him to kneel between my legs, and as he did so, I put one foot up on my desk to give him better access. He placed a couple of gentle kisses over the top of my panties, and I could feel my wetness increasing at the feel of his warm breath. He kissed up and down and all around the edges of my panties and over the gusset. Finally, as my breathing was becoming labored, he used his teeth to pull my panties down and then his hands to take them all the way over my knees and off my feet.

I loved the feeling of being in control, and I couldn't believe how easily he was doing everything I asked. I felt his lips gently suck my clit into his mouth and let out an involuntary moan. He flicked his tongue and made slow and deliberate circles over the tip. I closed my eyes and concentrated on the feeling. He finally released me and started to make long licks from my wet hole all the way up to back up to my clit. I was becoming engrossed in the feeling, and all the tension of the day was slipping away.

He circled my cunt a couple of times, and then I felt his skilled tongue making its way towards my ass. He took a firm hold of my thighs and pushed them up so that both of my feet were on the chair and my butt was on the edge. He began to alternate between firm kisses and gentle bites of my ass. I could feel the sensation throughout my entire body. My heartbeat was increasing, and my breathing was becoming deeper. Suddenly, his tongue found my asshole and he began to make little circles around it with his wet tongue. My breathing was loud now, and he knew I was enjoying it. Every so often, he would look up at me and then look back to the task in hand. He was using his thumb to stimulate my clit now, and the combination of sensations he was making from my ass and my clit was amazing.

Finally, Luke stiffened his tongue and penetrated my asshole. At the same time, he brought his thumb down and slipped it easily into my cunt. The upward motion of his thumb was hitting me in just the right spot, and I couldn't stop my hips from jerking up and down. I was close to my orgasm and ordering him not to stop. He kept his tongue in my ass and was moving it around in small circles.

"Ahhh yeah... Don't stop Luke... If you stop your fucking fired."

I heard my own voice call out and was totally getting off on the power I had over him. I felt my body begin to spasm. My asshole tightened around his tongue and pussy contracted around his thumb. My orgasm shattered through my body and I pulled him up to meet my face. I kissed his mouth deep and tasted a mixture of my ass and pussy juices. I loved it.

"Now you're going to fuck me with this lovely hard cock of yours."

I stood up and lent over my desk, keeping a firm hold of his cock. I hitched my skirt higher up my waist and guided him into my pussy from behind. As he entered my wet pussy, he let out a deep growl close to my ear.

"Your pussy feels so good."

I smiled but silenced him. "Shut up and fuck me."

With that, he slowly withdrew his cock until only the tip of the head was left inside. He held the shaft and began to move the head in circles around the entrance of my cunt. I knew he was trying to tease me, and it was starting to work.

"Fuck me or you're fired."

I knew he was smiling, but by this point, he needed it as much as I did. He grabbed hold of my waist, and with one firm movement, he thrust deep inside of me and began to fuck me hard and fast. He was bent over me now and brought his hand up to squeeze my tits over my shirt. His face was close to the back of my neck, and I could feel his breath on my skin. All of the sensations together were bringing me close, and I could feel from his labored breath that he was getting there too. I stuck my ass out further so his cock hit me deeper, and after another couple of thrusts, I could feel my orgasm building in my body. I was moaning pretty loud by now, which was only turning Luke on more, encouraging him to pound me harder and harder. All of a sudden, my body had gone into spasm once again, and my pussy was contracting around his cock. With a final groan, I felt Luke's sperm filling my hole.

We stayed in that position for a few seconds. Luke's hands on the edge of the desk for support. His softening his cock was still in my pussy, and his head was resting on my back. I allowed him to get his breath back, secretly planning the next opportunity I would have to abuse my power like this again.

6 WHIPPING IT UP

Fern lay on her bed and opened up her laptop. She was thinking about the events of the previous night as she entered the website address of her favorite porn site. Last night she had made love to her husband David, as they do on a fairly regular basis. After 8 years of marriage, they knew what each other enjoyed and most importantly how to get each other off. During the last few months though, Fern had been feeling as though something was missing. In the early days, there had been so much passion, so much fire, and they couldn't get enough of each other. Recently it had felt monotonous and boring, and despite always reaching orgasm, Fern was feeling less and less satisfied.

Last night was no exception; after sliding into bed next to Fern, David had put one arm around her and began to play with her nipples. He knew she had sensitive nips and would quickly become turned on, so this was often the way their lovemaking would begin. After a few minutes of kissing and fondling her body, she reached down and stroked his cock until he was hard. Fern knew the kind of strokes he liked—slow and firm movements up and down and a soft stroke of the head of his penis with her thumb as she reached the top. Once he was hard, he pulled her on top of him where she rode him until they both came. This was their favorite position and most of the time they would cum together.

Feeling a little guilty and thinking about Dave who would be at the office by now, Fern clicked on a video featuring a young couple that was already naked and kissing passionately. Instantly Fern reached for her nipples with one hand and began to stroke her inner thighs with the other. She imagined that it was Dave's hands touching her as she always did when she masturbated and kept her eyes on the computer whilst her hands explored her body. Even immediately after her orgasm the previous night, Fern hadn't felt completely satisfied and had been waiting for this opportunity to give her pussy some more of the attention that she was craving. The woman in the video was now sucking the man's cock. Fern brought her hand up to gently brush her fingertips over her slit and could already feel through her underwear that her pussy was moist. She loved to watch women sucking cock and always looked closely for new techniques that she could try on her Dave, not that she needed it. Fern knew how much her husband loved her blowjobs and she loved to give them just as much.

As she became more aroused, Fern slipped off her panties and reached for the dildo that she had placed next to her. She slipped two fingers into her pussy and slowly massaged her inner walls, feeling her wetness increasing. After a few minutes, she slid her fingers out and replaced them with her favorite dildo. It wasn't her biggest toy and didn't come close to reaching the same girth of Dave, but it had a nice curve to it that Fern found to always hit the spot. When it came to getting the feeling of her pussy being filled, no toy could do it as well as Dave, but right now, all she needed was an intense orgasm.

As Fern began to work the toy in and out of her pussy, the woman in the video brought out a leather whip. Fern noticed for the first time that the man was bound to the bed and the woman was now whipping her partner across the thighs and stomach. Fern increased the pace with which she was fucking herself; she found herself increasingly turned on as she imagined herself in the woman's position and Dave tied to the bed mercilessly. Fern bit her bottom lip as she brought her other hand down and began to make little circles over her clit. The feeling of both her clit and her G-spot being stimulated simultaneously was enough to bring her orgasm closer and her body began to writhe in expectation. She closed her eyes and enjoyed the sensation as she felt the wave of orgasm begin to roll over her body. As she came, she let out a long groan that signified her release of tension. Fern removed the dildo from her pussy and subconsciously made little circles with her fingertips around her cunt, enjoying the slippery wetness. As her breathing came back to normal, she heard the moans coming from the laptop and brought a hand up to close it, pausing for a moment before she did so to take another look at the whip and arm restraints that the couple were using. She shut the computer and then closed her eyes to go back to sleep for a while.

Fern woke up feeling energized and excited. She had already decided that she was going to go into town and purchase some items to help spice up her and her husband's sex life. She considered phoning Dave to run her idea past him first but quickly decided better of it. David was open-minded and Fern was sure he would be up for this. It would be all the more fun to surprise him with it. As she walked to the bathroom, she stopped in the full-length mirror and looked her body up and down. She had long strawberry blonde hair and a decent figure. At 36 years old, her D-cup breasts weren't as perky as she remembered and her once perfectly toned belly was now covered with a thin layer of flab. Overall, though Fern knew she still looked pretty good and made a mental note to herself to pick up some new sexy underwear whilst she was out. She took a quick shower, got dressed and headed off to town.

Dave arrived home from work at about 6:30PM and found his wife in the kitchen making dinner. The dining room table was made up with a rose in the vase in the center, and his first instinct was that he had forgotten some kind of anniversary or Valentine's Day. He quickly thought about what the date was and was sure that it was nothing special. He walked up to his wife from behind and wrapped his arms around her.

"What's all this?" he asked.

Fern smiled as she felt him approach her from behind. She loved the feeling of his body close to hers and always felt so safe when nestling in his large frame. She turned around and looked at her husband.

"Just wanted to do something nice for you!" As she said this, she lifted her skirt a little to reveal some red suspenders. "Go take a shower whilst I finish dinner." She gave him a sly smile and turned back to the stove.

Dave stood smiling in the same spot for a couple of seconds, wondering what had gotten into his wife before heading off to the bathroom, removing his suit jacket as he did so.

Fern tried to concentrate on finishing dinner but her heart was already beating a little faster than usual thinking about how her husband was going to react. Ever since she had come back from town, Fern had been getting increasingly horny as her mind continued to play over what she had planned for the evening. Now that he was home from work, she wasn't even sure if she would be able to get through dinner before pouncing on him and having her way with him.

Just as she was serving up, Dave walked back into the dining room wearing some casual shorts and a shirt. "Sorry I didn't have anything to wear as sexy as what you have!"

"Don't worry. You're not going to be wearing anything for long!"

Dave laughed at his wife's comment and once again wondered what had happened to her. They had a very easy and comfortable sex life, but it was rare for her to take the lead and be so forward like this. He was quite enjoying it and felt a little twitch in his pants at the thought of how the evening was going to go.

The couple ate dinner with the normal chitchat about their day but all with a slight sexual undertone. Dave kept thinking about what the rest of his wife's new underwear looks like, while Fern was thinking about the handcuffs that were awaiting them upstairs. They finished dinner and Fern walked around the table to take David's plate away when he grabbed her by the waist and tried to pull her into him. She laughed and tried to resist and fight him off as his hands fumbled for the zip at the back of her skirt. Fern wanted to be in control tonight so she grabbed his hands and started to lead him upstairs.

When they reached the bedroom, Fern turned to David and gave him a passionate kiss on the lips. They stood embraced, enjoying the familiar feeling and taste of each other's lips. When David's hands began to wander to Fern's ass, groping her and trying to lift up her skirt, she pushed him backwards until he fell onto the bed. She climbed on top of him and continued to kiss him, sucking his tongue into her mouth and nibbling on his bottom lip. All of the time his hands were feeling around her body, trying to grasp her ass or reach up under her blouse, but every time he got close, she would grab his arms and put them back flat against his body. She could feel him smiling under her lips and knew that he was enjoying her dominance.

Continuing the kiss and holding his attention to it, Fern slid her hand under one of the pillows and pulled something out from underneath. She broke the kiss and David opened his eyes to see her holding a blindfold. Fern gently raised his head from the bed and he simply smiled as she put it on him, softly kissing each eyelid before shielding his view. Once his eyes were covered, she continued to kiss him, first on the lips and then all over his face before turning her attention to his neck. His hands were becoming more and more troublesome, desperately trying to feel her breasts.

"I'm going to have to do something about these roaming hands of yours." Fern breathed softly into his ear. As she did so, she reached under the pillow again. David felt something embrace his wrist and then Fern moved his arm up so that his hand was close to the head of the bed. He realized that she had handcuffed him to the railing. Fern did the same thing to the other hand, all the time watching the smile creeping across her husband's face.

"You're bad!" she heard him say. She planted a few more kisses on his neck and then sat up. She could feel his hard-on poking into her and was becoming eager to see it. She unbuttoned his shirt, kissing down his body after each button revealed more flesh. Finally, she slid it off him and took off his shorts. She whispered in his ear, "I'll be right back," and left the room.

Fern returned with a bowl of ice and opened the drawer to take out her newly purchased leather whip. She took a moment to admire her husband's naked form. She loved the sight of him with his arms restrained above his body and his hard cock pointing upwards waiting for some attention. She couldn't wait to taste it too but first she wanted to have a go with her new toy. She kneeled on the bed next to her husband and kissed him deeply. Then she sat up and began to brush the whip gently down his body, starting at his chest and slowly bringing it down to tickle over his cock and then down his thighs all the way to his feet. She repeated this a few times, working up the courage to actually whip him. Finally, she did it, starting at his ankles, as she wasn't sure how he would react and didn't want to surprise him too much.

"Haha, oww, is that a whip?"

"Yep," Fern replied, whipping him again, this time on the thighs as she had seen his light-hearted reaction.

"Mmmm," he moaned, giving her permission to continue. She focused on his thighs and stomach but never hit him in the same place twice. She did it slowly, always waiting a different amount of time between strokes, so he never knew exactly when or where he would be struck. Fern could see his cock twitching with anticipation and beads of precum were beginning to appear on the tip of his cock. When red marks began to appear on his body, Fern put the whip down and picked up a cube of ice. She started on his stomach, dragging the ice slowly along the red lines she had made. He began to moan again, his body flinching slightly each time she put the ice on a new place on his hot body. She followed the trail of ice she was leaving with gentle kisses.

After his stomach, she moved to his inner things, working the ice up towards his groin. She would get close to his cock but never touch it, loving the way it moved involuntarily. Finally, when she couldn't resist the beautiful sight any longer, she put the ice cube on the base and moved it slowly to the head. As soon as it touched the tip, she replaced the cold ice cube with her warm mouth and sucked the entire shaft inside, flicking and circling her tongue around the head at the same time. Dave let out one of the loudest and most genuine groans she had ever heard him make. She knew her pussy would be soaking wet by now by the way it was throbbing, desperate for some attention. She straddled one of Dave's legs grinding up and down. Having some contact with her pussy was enough to start Fern moaning as she continued to hump his leg whilst moaning and move her mouth up and down on his cock. He was going to cum soon and Fern knew it by the way his hips were beginning to rise in an attempt to keep as much of his cock in her mouth as possible.

"Ahhh, I'm going to cum, love." When she heard her husband's words, Fern took a breath and then bent down, taking his whole shaft into her mouth until her lips were firmly wrapped around his cock. She knew how much he loved to finish in her mouth and it was only a moment or two before she felt his cum hitting the back of her throat. She released his cock and kissed her way up to his body. She removed the blindfold and the couple kissed deeply. She looked at her husband, removed her top, and then stood up over him to let her skirt drop. She stayed there for a while, allowing Dave to take in the sight of her sexy new underwear. The panties were crotchless so from this position, he was looking straight at her bare pussy.

"Undo the handcuffs, love. Now it's my turn to fuck you."

"Nope! Not today... Today I'm in charge."

She stepped forward so that she was straddling his face and slowly began to lower herself over him. She got to a few inches above his face and then stopped. She could see him trying to raise his head to reach her, but the handcuffs wouldn't allow him to. She smiled and he looked her in the eyes.

"Come on! I wanna taste you... please!"

She couldn't hold out any longer; more than anything Fern needed some attention to her pussy. She lowered herself further and moaned loudly when David's tongue came to suckle on her clit. She moved her hips in circles over his mouth, controlling the pressure in just the way she liked it. She alternated her position so that sometimes the focus was on her clit and at others, he was fucking her hole with his tongue. It felt amazing but finally she needed more. She reached behind her to find that his cock was already hard again. She moved backwards down his body and positioned his cock at the entrance of her cunt. Fern teased him a little by letting only the head touch her and moving in circles, barely letting him inside of her. She was teasing herself as much as him, so she finally sat down, allowing his thick cock to fill her up. They both groaned at the sensation and Fern immediately began to ride him hard and fast, suddenly desperate for some release. They were moaning together louder and louder and Fern was fucking Dave harder than ever before, enjoying each deep thrust of his cock in her cunt.

Finally she felt her whole body tense as she exploded, causing Dave to cum for the second time. Fern collapsed on top of him and that is where she stayed until she had recovered enough to roll off of him before they both fell into a deep and satisfied sleep.

7 TEACHING HER A LESSON

Vicky walked in late, as usual. I don't know about the attendance for her other classes, but she's usually late for mine. She closed the door behind her and flashed me an easy smile that she knew made it hard to discipline her.

"Sorry, Mr. Scott."

She sounded so sweet and innocent.

"Just take a seat, Vicky, and find your work from last lesson."

"Yes, Sir."

She walked right in front of my desk and over to her seat in the middle of the room. I couldn't help but notice her legs as she walked past me. She was wearing a ridiculously short skirt accompanied by a tight fitting shirt. I was aware of some of the guys in the class leering at her long legs and mentally scolded myself for being as weak as they are.

There are many attractive girls around the campus, but I'd never experienced any actual desire for any of them. Vicky was different. She was a smart student and when she had the motivation to knuckle down, she always produced good work. The difficult part was getting her motivated and to get her to actually show up to lessons.

She often caused problems in the classroom – which meant that I was regularly asking her to stay behind for little "chats," during which I would attempt to address her bad behavior and attendance. As a result of these after lesson chats, I probably knew her the best out of all of my students. We had developed some kind of understanding. I never came down on her really hard like many of the other teachers did. I tried to help her. I had a genuine interest in trying to help her get her grades up and improve her situation, and she had responded by not giving me quite so much attitude during my lessons and at least attempting to do the work.

I'm a fairly young teacher at 24. This is only my second year working. I think it helps being young as a teacher because you have a better understanding and memory of what it's like to be that age.

The negative side, of course, is that with such a small age gap, it can be hard to gain their respect. At first, I thought Vicky was listening and responding to me because I was talking to her on her level. Now I'm fairly sure she's attracted to me. I don't think that's too abnormal for a student to have a crush on a teacher. I'm starting to find myself looking at her in an inappropriate way for a teacher to look at a student.

I was trying to keep my eyes on some of the papers on my desk, but I heard some rustling by her desk and looked over. She hadn't sat down, but has instead decided to take her time taking the books out of her bag. As I glanced over, she was bent over with her bag on the floor and ass in the air. I didn't know if she assumed this position consciously, but her ass was pointing directly towards me with her skirt riding up higher and higher. It took all of my energy to look away and appear unflustered. I cleared my throat and continued to conduct the lesson that I had previously planned, all of the time trying to concentrate on the work and not look over at Vicky too much.

This particular lesson was on poetry, which, I have to admit, is not one of the aspects of the subject that I find most interesting. I know the students are struggling with it as well. After asking the class what their interpretation of a particular poem was, Vicky piped up.

"This is bullshit, Sir! Why do we need to learn this stuff? We're never going to use it."

"You never know what knowledge will come in useful in the future. Just learn it, Vicky, pass your exams with a good grade and your whole world will open up."

"Wow, you make it sound so romantic, Sir."

This would have sounded innocent enough coming from someone else. When Vicky said it, it seemed to have an underlying meaning. I felt my cheeks getting warm, so I quickly repeated the question and prompted a different student to answer. I got through the lesson and as everyone was packing up their belongings, I asked Vicky to stay behind for a moment. I couldn't have her calling out in class all the time, using bad language and making inappropriate remarks.

I was at the back of the room collecting some papers and then turned to walk back to the front of the room. Vicky was sitting in my chair behind my desk.

"You wanted to see me, Sir." She smiled as she spun from side to side on my wheelie chair. She looked so sexy at that moment. All I could do to keep myself from smiling was to maintain my stern expression. I walked quickly over to her and told her to stand up. The classroom door was open, and for some reason I felt nervous about her sitting in my chair; it was too informal for a student to look so comfortable and at home in my seat.

I stood right next to her now and hissed under my breath, "Vicky, stand up now." Her smile disappeared and she suddenly looked sad and confused, not really knowing what she had done wrong. At seeing her upset, I automatically dropped my defenses and wanted to console her.

"Sorry, I didn't mean to sound so angry."

I brushed my fingertips over her hand, which was resting on the arm of my chair. I was looking into her eyes to see if she was okay. It was only when she dropped her eyes to look at my hand on top of hers that I realized it was still there, and I was gently stroking the top of her hand.

"Sorry...I... just....I didn't mean to upset you."

"No, it's fine."

I stood directly in front of her now, and we had found ourselves in a strange almost intertwining position. She sat down with her knees bent and opened slightly, whilst I was standing with my legs opened slightly and one of her knees was between my legs. I saw her eyes drop down to look at my crotch, which was a mere inch from her knee. She raised her leg ever so slowly until her knee gently met me. I felt some slight pressure on my balls, and then she started to move her knee in circles so she was gently massaging me.

"Vicky, what are you doing?" I tried to sound serious but my voice cracked, and I didn't move a muscle, clearly giving her permission to continue. The massaging of my balls combined with the danger and excitement of the situation meant that it wasn't long before I started to get hard. Vicky's eyes were alternating from watching the growing lump in my pants to looking me right in the eyes.

She was looking at me so deeply it was as if she was trying to see what I was thinking. I don't really know what I was thinking other than, "You should stop this before anything really happens."

One of her hands was still under mine, but I saw the other one lift off of the chair arm and move towards my increasing erection. She put her whole palm flat on top of my cock and began to make circles with it, mirroring the action she was doing with her knee. I closed my eyes for a moment as I couldn't help but enjoy the feeling of some attention to my cock. Her palm was now cupped slightly around my cock, and Vicky changed the motion to up and down movements so that she was practically now jerking me off through my trousers. Every now and then, I would glance up at the open door, but as it was the end of the day, it was fairly quiet outside. The rest of the time, I was watching her face, loving how interested she had become in my hard-on. I'm sure this would be the biggest cock she had ever played with as she was looking more and more impressed as it continued to grow bigger and harder in her hand. I must admit seeing how impressed she was made the whole situation even more erotic for me.

I felt her hands begin to fondle with my zip, and I realized that she was trying to get access to my cock. Something finally triggered in my mind, and I knew I couldn't let her go any further.

"Vicky, no."

I pulled my zip back up and she quickly resumed playing with me over my pants. I don't know why I let her carry out. In my mind I tried to rationalize it, thinking that skin on skin contact was going too far, but through the pants wasn't so bad.

She grabbed my hand and put it on one of her tits. Again, it was over clothes so some fucked up voice in my head was telling me that it was ok. I squeezed her firm tit and she looked up at me, slightly opening her mouth and licking her parted lips. I knew I wanted to fuck her before, but this was the first time I had a strong desire to kiss her. I was just about to lean in to kiss her when I heard a door close next door, and the sound of footsteps walking towards us in the corridor. My brain kicked in just in time, and I stepped away and leant over the desk as if reading a document with Vicky just as Mrs. Brown, one of my colleagues stuck her head around the corner to remind me about a department meeting.

"Yep, I'll be right there."

I was attempting to sound as normal as possible. I stood motionless for a few moments as I listened to her footsteps walk away.

"Fuck! That was too close. This will never happen again, Vicky, do you understand?"

My tone was a little too aggressive, as I really should never have let it happen.

"Why not?"

"Because I'm your teacher! This is wrong and we will face major consequences if we get caught."

I felt sweaty and panicky and my heart was beating faster than ever before. Then I looked at her face and saw that she was smiling. I took a few breaths and tried to calm down, realizing that we hadn't been caught and I needed to relax.

"Go on. Go home. See you in class next week and this never happened, ok?"

"Of course, Mr. Scott."

She looked at me in the eyes and before

I could turn away planted a soft kiss on my cheek. Then immediately she turned and walked out the door, leaving me staring at her ass as she went. I felt my cock twitch as I grabbed what I needed for the meeting and thought about how desperately I needed to get home and jerk off.

I was grateful that I had the weekend between our encounter and our next lesson together on Monday afternoon. I tried as much as possible to keep Vicky out of my mind, but every so often, I would realize that I was thinking about her and end up jerking off to the memory of her touching my cock in the classroom. All throughout Monday, I was dreading seeing her again, whilst part couldn't wait. When the bell rang for the start of fourth period, I was already behind my desk waiting for the students to come in. I was trying to be subtle but looking only for Vicky and felt a twinge of disappointment when she didn't turn up for the start of the lesson.

I realized inside that I naturally thought she would be excited and eager to see me again. "Fuck! Sort your head out," I told myself and attempted to get on with the lesson without turning to the door to see if it was her each time I heard a noise.

It was the end of the day and I walked over to my car thinking only about why she didn't show. Was she trying to make me miss her? Was she not as interested in me as I thought? Was she sick? I was beginning to piss myself off with the fact that I let one of my students get under my skin. I'm sure I had a face like thunder when I heard a voice come up behind me just as I opened my car door.

"So how was your day, Mr. Scott?"

I knew before I turned around that it was Vicky. I turned around with a smile before I had a chance to consider what to say or do. I managed to resist it but my instinct was screaming at me to give her a kiss, as if greeting a girlfriend.

"Any chance of a lift home?"

She was already walking to the passenger side. I smiled at her and got in the car.

We were making idle chitchat and were only a couple of minutes outside of the school when Vicky reached over and started feeling for my cock. This time she wasn't going to stay outside of the pants and quickly undid my zip and button to pull my cock out. She leaned over and put my whole cock in her mouth. It felt so good and I immediately began to get hard in her mouth.

"Oh my god, that's good!"

I tried to concentrate on driving and acted as if nothing out of the ordinary was happening whilst my hot English student sucked my cock. Once I was too big for her to keep in her mouth, she switched to long licks down either side of the shaft combined with some gentle sucking and flicking of the tongue on the tip.

"Mmmm. . . I can taste your cum . . . Does it feel good?"

"It feels great, Vicky, don't stop."

"Alright but don't cum, I want you to fuck me first."

I had been enjoying the blowjob so much that I hadn't considered what else might happen. The thought of fucking her turned me even more, and now all I could think about was where I should take her to fuck her. I thought about doing her in the back of the car but that seemed a little immature. If I was going to go through with this, I wanted to show her what it's like to be with a real man. I couldn't walk in to hotel with her, not in this town anyway, in case we're recognized. The only choice was back to my place, and hope that nobody saw. She still had her head in my lap. I was enjoying it a little too much, and I was surprised at how good she was.

I pulled up outside my house and we rushed inside. My boner was massive and clearly visible but I didn't want to wait. I needed to get inside and fuck her. There was a sparkle in Vicky's eyes as we entered my bedroom and she looked around. I closed the bedroom door and pushed her against it, kissing her deeply for the first time. We scrambled around and removed each other's clothes, both of us knowing exactly where this was heading.

"Damn! I want you to fuck me."

She moaned as I reached for her pussy, feeling her already soaking wet cunt. I slipped a finger inside and felt her tight pussy. She moaned out and I carried her over to the bed. I straddled her and lined my cock up with her hole. I wasn't sure how much experience she had had so I made sure to be gentle. I entered her slowly, taking in the sensations caused by the tightness of her pussy. She was so wet that my big cock slid in easily and her moans of enjoyment encouraged me to start thrusting into her. I put my head down and sucked on her nipples as I fucked her, slowly increasing the pace and thrusting harder. She was moaning louder than any girl I had ever fucked, and I was totally getting off on the sound of it. I was getting close and I wanted her to cum with me. I slowed down until I had nearly stopped and began to tease her by slowly pulling my cock nearly all of the way out and then fucking her deep in her pussy. She was moaning and groaning until finally she begged me.

"Fuck me, please! Make me cum."

I released her nipple and moved my head up to kiss her passionately on the lips. Then I gave her exactly what she wanted, what we both wanted, and began to fuck her hard and fast. It wasn't long before we were both moaning together, and after a few more minutes, we both climaxed. I filled her pussy with my cum and as I pulled my cock out, I saw it seeping out of her, mixed with her own juices.

I moved up the bed and collapsed next to her.

"Wow! You fuck really well, Sir."

"Thanks, Vicky, so do you. And by the way...I think you can call me Chris."

8 BATTLE OF HE HEART AND MIND PART 1

Connection

The three girls arrived at flat number 36 and Tina knocked on the door. "Are you sure it's not going to be full of lesbians?" Hannah asked her two friends with a worried look on her face. Her two best friends, Tina and Georgie, were both gay and although not technically a couple, did tend to hook up on a regular basis, especially on drunken nights such as this one was likely to be. Hannah had no problem hanging out with lesbians but often found herself stuck at some kind of lesbian event when she would much rather be utilizing her time looking for guys.

"Don't worry, there will be plenty of cock inside that you can get your lips around," Tina answered her and Hannah pulled a face. Yes, she liked men but she hated the vulgar language that Tina was so fond of and rarely talked about sex.

"That's disgusting Tina", Hannah replied.

"You don't need to tell me that it's disgusting!" Tina looked at Georgie and they both laughed.

"No honestly, I don't think Chloe is even gay is she, T?" Georgie asked Tina, in her role that she often assumed as the mediator of the group.

"No idea, I've never asked her," Tina replied. "I don't even know her that well."

"What the hell are we doing here then, I thought you were friends?"

"Well we kind of are, she's a friend of a friend and she said it's an open invitation, bring whoever you want. Come on, it's a party, it's gonna be fun!"

Just at that moment, the door opened and a girl with jet-black hair stood on the other side.

"Hey guys! Hey it's Tina, right?" The girl stepped forward and gave Tina a quick hug, and then introduced herself to the other two girls.

"Hey I'm Chloe, welcome to my place! Come on in and make yourself at home."

The three girls walked in and Tina

handed Chloe a bottle of Vodka as they were led to the kitchen for their first round of drinks.

"First drink for all guests is a shot of tequila, I'm afraid." Chloe informed them with a friendly smile on her face. She looked Hannah in the eyes as she handed her a shot glass and Hannah was mesmerized by the sparkling blue of Chloe's eyes. As their eye contact lingered for slightly longer than would normally be natural, they were interrupted by Georgie, who thanked their hostess for the invitation.

"Not a problem. Let me introduce you to some people." Chloe grabbed Hannah by the hand and gestured for Georgie and Tina to follow as they made their way into the living room. As Hannah looked around the room, she was pleased to see a mixture of both girls and guys. She really wished she wasn't holding Chloe's hand and hoped that nobody mistook her for a lesbian. Chloe seemed very nice and was certainly beautiful, but Hannah had never been interested in girls and she didn't want to get stuck with a label around these new people.

As Chloe introduced the three girls to some of her friends, Hannah once again found herself looking intently at Chloe. She had an energy about her that seemed to draw people in and make them feel relaxed. And she had such a friendly and comfortable manner that you instantly felt relaxed in her company. She was struck once again by Chloe's eyes, the sparkling blue and the way they contrasted against the dark hair. She was wearing a dress that came to just below her knees but had a slit that revealed a fair bit of thigh on one leg. Hannah admired the dress and thought Chloe looked incredibly sexy in it. She checked out the hostess' legs and considered how flawless her skin was. She had a natural looking tan, and her skin looked so silky and soft that anyone would have had a desire to reach out and feel the smoothness. Suddenly, she realized that she hadn't been following the conversation and Tina and Georgie were walking off somewhere.

"Don't worry; they're just going to the bathroom." Chloe caught her, just as she was about to run after them. "Stay with me," she said with a genuine smile that instantly made Hannah relax. "How about another shot?" Chloe said to the little group they had joined.

"Sounds great!" Hannah answered. She knew once she had some alcohol in her system she would relax a bit more. Hannah always felt somewhat nervous in social situations, especially when she didn't know anyone. Someone arrived with a tray full of tequila shots, lime, and salt and everyone reached for one. They all said cheers and clinked glasses, Hannah and Chloe making eye contact once again, just before they both downed their shots and took a bite of lime. After that, normal friendly conversation between the groups continued. Georgie and Tina came back to join everyone and the party got going.

A little while later, the alcohol was really flowing and everyone had had a fair bit to drink. Hannah had really relaxed into the party and was chatting comfortably with various people at the party. She looked around the room in search of Georgie and Tina and spotted them dancing in the middle of the room. Tina was dancing behind Georgie with her hands on her hips while Georgie grinded up and down in front of Tina. Hannah watched as Tina's hands came up to play with Georgie's tits while Georgie's hands wrapped around Tina's waist pulling her close and squeezing her ass as the same time. Tina was the more masculine of the two and Hannah mused over how they always ended up dancing in this position. Also, it was a sure sign that they would end up fucking at some point that night, and Hannah wondered why they never admitted their true feelings for each other and become an item. It was obvious that they both wanted to but when sober they both denied it, claiming to love the single lifestyle too much. She watched on as Tina spun Georgie around so that they were face to face and brought her in as they embraced and shared a fiery kiss on the lips. Their hands were all over each other as they continued to kiss and dance to the music.

Hannah poured herself another drink and then took a seat on an empty armchair, cheerily looking around the room at everyone enjoying themselves talking and dancing.

"How you doing there?" All of a sudden Chloe was sitting on the arm of the chair next to Hannah with her arm around her.

"I'm good, just taking a break from dancing."

"Yeah, it's getting kind of hot in here. Especially over there!" Chloe gestured over to the middle of the room where Tina and Georgie were enjoying a full on kiss. Hannah laughed.

"So what's going on with them? Are they together?" Chloe asked, so Hannah filled her in on their history of drunken one night flings and mutual denial of wanting to be in a relationship. Chloe listened intently, watching Hannah's lips as she spoke, partly because she couldn't hear very well over the music and partly because she was mesmerized by Hannah's soft pink lips, currently covered in a shiny lip balm. When Hannah paused from telling the story to take a sip of her drink, Chloe noticed some of her lip-gloss smudge. She instinctively put her finger up to wipe the color from under Hannah's lip. Hannah was caught slightly off guard as she wasn't expecting it, but as Chloe's hand gently brushed over her lip, she felt herself lean in to increase the contact. Their eyes meet as they had a number of times over the night and Chloe slowly took her hand away.

They both took another sip of their drinks, almost to break the tension. Hannah suddenly felt awkward, she enjoyed the tenderness of Chloe's touch on her face, and in the moment, she wanted it to last longer. I must have had too much to drink, Hannah thought. Part of her wished Chloe would go and talk to someone else so that the awkwardness of the moment would go away but another part of her was really hoping she would stay. Throughout the night, Hannah had thoroughly enjoyed the company of Chloe and, despite having only just met her, had a strong feeling that she wanted to get to know her more.

"So how about you?"

Hannah was so relieved and thankful to Chloe for breaking the silence. "How about me what?"

"Do you have a partner? Boyfriend, girlfriend?"

"Oh," now she felt a bit shy again. "Erm no, I don't. I'm single. How about you?"

"I'm single too. Broke up with my girlfriend about 6 months ago."

"Oh, I...I'm sorry to hear that."

"Oh don't be, she was crazy. I'm so pleased to be out of that relationship! So can I ask you a question, I've been trying to figure something out all night. Are you into girls or guys?"

"Oh, I'm not gay. I like guys. I just don't have a boyfriend at the moment." Chloe smiled when she saw how defensive Hannah got about it.

"Well...that's a shame."

"What's a shame?" Hannah asked feeling a little nervous about the whole conversation, especially now that she knew Chloe was a lesbian.

"Just that you're very cute and I thought we got along well. Also I felt like maybe you might like me a little bit!" Chloe looked Hannah right in the eye as she said this, hoping to see her true reaction. Hannah simply blushed and looked down at her drink.

"Sorry, I'm not a lesbian," was all Hannah could think to say. Chloe just laughed and changed the conversation, not wanting to make Hannah feel uncomfortable. They soon settled back into their comfortable conversation and found themselves talking and getting to know each other like old friends.

Finally, a loud crash of thunder made Hannah and Chloe stop talking, and as they looked around the room, they noticed that the flat was almost empty. They had been so engrossed in their conversation that they hadn't noticed the rest of the guests leave. On the other side of the room, Tina and Georgie were also blissfully unaware of the rest of the party. They were clearly getting more and more turned on as the grinding had become more forceful and more necessary, and their hands were wandering all over each other as they enjoyed the taste of each other's mouth. Hannah walked over to them and feeling a little bad to interrupt managed to get their attention.

"Come on guys, we should probably make a move. It's getting late and everyone else had gone!"

Chloe walked over to join them. "You should take a look outside first. It's pouring down. Why don't the three of you spend the night here and then go home in the morning when the rain has stopped?"

Tina and Georgie looked at each other. They were clearly trying to figure out what to do, as they were desperate to fuck but also didn't want to venture out in the middle of a storm. "Don't worry guys, I have a spare room. You guys can sleep in there and Hannah can stay in my room."

They all agreed but Chloe could see that Hannah felt uncomfortable with the situation. "Don't worry Hannah, I'll sleep on the couch; I normally pass out here anyway when I'm drunk!"

Hannah smiled at Chloe appreciating the offer. "Don't be silly, come on we can share a bed." So the four girls said goodnight and headed off to their rooms.

Tina and Georgie walked hand in hand to the guest bedroom. As soon as they got in there, Tina shut the door and pressed Georgie up against it. She took her face in her hands and kissed her firmly on the lips. Her hands gently played with Georgie's long, blonde, curly hair. As the kiss broke Tina moved down, planting kisses on Georgie's neck, making her way down to her cleavage. When she reached the edge of her top, she pulled Georgie away from the door and lifted her shirt over her head. She threw it on the floor and then knelt down to undo the buttons of her shorts. As she did so, Tina was planting soft little kisses on her belly just above the edge of her jeans. Georgie was beginning to moan out loud, and when Tina pulled her shorts down to her ankles and off her feet, she knew her wetness would already be seeping through her panties. They had had sex before so Georgie knew how good Tina was with her tongue. The anticipation had been building up all night as she waited for this moment, when she would feel Tina's tongue on her pussy again.

Tina went straight for Georgie's hole and began to kiss and suck the juices that were seeping through her panties. When she decided she wanted a real taste of her friends wet pussy, she used her teeth to slide her underwear down. Not willing to waste a second longer, she dove straight in, fucking Georgie's tight hole with her tongue. Once she had had a good taste, she began to kiss up her inner lips making little circles around Georgie's clit. Georgie's hips were now moving too in an effort to create contact between her clit and Tina's lips. Tina knew she was teasing her friend, and when she looked up, she saw pleading eyes staring back at her. She gave in and quickly flicked her tongue over Georgie's clit before sucking it in. At feeling this Georgie moaned out loud.

"Fuck yeah, T! I love it when you lick my pussy."

"Mmm you taste so good," Tina said before returning to take the little nub back into her mouth. She loved to fuck girls and there was nothing she loved more than licking Georgie out just the way she liked it. She loved to hear her friend moan.

She worked her tongue faster and faster over her clit, and when Georgie put her hands on Tina's head to keep her in place, she knew that she was close to getting her friend off. She licked furiously, alternating between firm strokes and soft circles until she felt the muscles in her friend's stomach begin to tense. She took Georgie's clit into her mouth one last time and sucked on it while Georgie rode out her orgasm, moaning loudly the entire time.

Hannah and Chloe climbed into bed fully clothed and pulled the blanket over them. What with the weather outside, the air had become quite chilly. Hannah let her head drop onto the pillow and felt her body relax. She was feeling a little tipsy and was relieved that she didn't have to go outside and weather the storm. She wasn't bothered at all the presence of Chloe lying next to her and was actually quite enjoying the warmth that she could feel radiating off of her body. Just as she was closing her eyes, Hannah heard a noise coming from next door. At first, she couldn't tell what it was but then she heard it again. This time louder and followed by the words "Ah fuck, yeah" and she realized she was hearing her best friends having sex.

"Oh God!" Hannah mumbled. "They're so loud! I'm so sorry!" Hannah looked over to Chloe to see her trying to suppress a laugh. The look on her face made Hannah laugh out loud, which was enough to push Chloe too far and she exploded with laughter. Both girls had an infectious laugh, which was only spurring each other on. After a good 5 minutes of belly laughing, they were shocked out of it by a massive clap of thunder. Hannah jumped and looked worrying towards the window as she saw a flash of lighting from behind the curtains.

"I hate thunder and lightning. Scares the shit out of me."

"Oh, you'll be fine." Just as Chloe said it, there was a second clash and she saw Hannah jump again.

"Come over here." Chloe put her arm out and gestured for Hannah to come closer. Hannah did so and rested her head on the space between Chloe's shoulder and her chest. She could feel her heart beat and instantly felt safe. Hannah let her eyes fall heavily and when she sensed another clap of thunder somewhere in the distance, she felt Chloe's arms hold her tight. The two girls slept peacefully, spending the entire night in each other's arms.

9 BATTLE OF THE HEART AND MIND PART 2

Inevitable

The four girls were casually browsing around the shopping mall one Saturday afternoon. Tina, Georgie, and Hannah have been best friends for years, but Chloe was a fairly new addition to the close friendship group. Ever since they first met at Chloe's party a couple of weeks back, Hannah and Chloe's friendship had continued to grow. After they shared a bed together keeping each other safe through a thunderstorm, it was as though they had a special bond. Georgie nudged Tina in the ribs and gestured for her to look over to where the other two girls appeared to be having some kind of play fight at the other side of the shop. "Look at those two. They look like a married couple!"

"Don't get me started on them. I don't know why they can't see what's happening!"

Georgie and Tina have been watching the relationship between the two girls develop with great interest. Hannah, who has never had any interest in girls, denies flat out that there is anything going on between her and Chloe other than a strong friendship. Chloe who is an out and proud lesbian claims to have been attracted to Hannah at the beginning but is now happy to have her as a good friend. To Georgie, Tina, and the rest of the world, the nature of their relationship was obvious but the two in question as of yet remained in denial.

"Anyway I better be getting to work." Tina was the manager of a bar in town. "You coming with me or staying here?"

"Oh come on, you can't leave me with these two, I feel like a third wheel."

"Alright then. Hey guys!" Georgie called over to the other two, "I'm taking Tina to work, catch you later."

Hannah and Chloe waved goodbye to their friends and continued browsing. "That shirt looks cute." Hannah said reaching for an item on a railing above her head. "Awwww!"

"What's up?"

"I don't know, the top of my back has been stiff and I just felt a twinge in my neck."

"I've told you before; let me give you a massage. It's on the house and I guarantee it will sort you out." Chloe said, offering her services as a professional masseuse.

"I know I just feel bad. You give massages all day..."

Hannah had always been a very thoughtful and considerate person, never wanting anyone to go to any trouble for her. Chloe thought about this as she listened to her new friend and thought that this was one of the many reasons why she liked her so much. One of the other reasons was her beautiful face and curly blonde hair, but Chloe kept this to herself, as she knew it was best not to go there again. The two girls had had a deep conversation the night they met, and Chloe had realized there and then that if she wanted Hannah in her life, it would have to be as a friend. Since that night, she's kept her true feelings to herself, out of fear of losing the first girl she has ever felt an immediate and intense connection to.

"You don't want to be giving out freebies in your free time," Hannah continued.

"Don't you think that's up to me? Come on, I don't like seeing you in pain, let me help you!"

"Fine!"

"Great! Let's do it this evening when we get back."

Once they were bored with shopping, Hannah and Chloe grabbed a quick snack and headed back to Chloe's place. When they got back, Hannah stuck the TV on and took a seat on the sofa; she had been spending so much time as Chloe's recently that Hannah felt like it was her second home. Chloe went into the guest bedroom and got everything prepared for the massage. Even though it was a freebie for a friend, she was determined to make it just as good as she would for a client. She wanted to come across professional and of course, she also wanted Hannah to benefit from it. Once she set up the table, she called Hannah in to the guest bedroom and told her to get undressed. "How naked should I be?" Hannah asked innocently. Chloe couldn't help a grin spreading across her face, but the two were comfortable enough with each other now to be able to make jokes and flirt innocently with each other so Hannah didn't mind. In fact Hannah loved to see Chloe smile, and sometimes if she hadn't seen her for a day or two, she physically missed the sight of her friends smile.

"The more naked the better is all I'm gonna say."

Hannah laughed at her friend's unsubtle flirting. Chloe threw a towel at her and told she would wait outside until she was ready.

After a few minutes, Chloe knocked on the door and then let herself in. Hannah was lying face down on the table with a towel over her ass. Chloe was surprised to see that Hannah had taken her bra off; despite the easy joking, she had expected all underwear to be kept on. Chloe had already turned on some soft background music and lit a couple of incense sticks, and Hannah was already feeling comfortable and relaxed.

"There's a danger that I could fall asleep here." Chloe heard Hannah's muffled voice come from under the table.

"Just relax!"

Chloe drizzled some massage oil over Hannah's back and then rubbed some into her hands. She had been a qualified masseuse for years and she knew she was good. But finally being able to get her hands on Hannah made her feel both nervous and excited, and Chloe noted to herself that her heart was beating harder and faster than usual. She began the massage starting on Hannah's upper back and shoulders, which is where her muscles were stiff. She worked the muscles hard concentrating on her technique and really trying to locate all of the knots in her friends back. Every so often, she would hear Hannah purr with enjoyment. While she appreciated the acknowledgement that she was doing a good job, she was also finding the noise erotic and was aware that she was becoming turned on. As she continued to work her way down Hannah's back, she was finding it harder to ignore her growing arousal.

Chloe's thumbs were sliding down the muscles in her lower back towards the edge of the towel that was covering her ass. She let her thumbs slip a little way under the towel and was relieved when she heard Hannah continue to purr every now and then. After a little while it was time to move on to the legs, so Chloe walked down to the end of the table to start with the feet. Once again, everything started okay and Chloe kept her mind busy by concentrating on her technique. Hannah was still making the occasional noise though, and as Chloe made her way higher up her legs, it was becoming more frequent. She was now sliding her fingers up the inside of Hannah's thighs, starting at the inner knee and going all the way up, very close to her pussy.

Chloe knew this move felt good but she

did it nervously to start with, unsure as to whether Hannah would think she is going too far and be angry with her or not. Her first sign that it was safe to continue was when her fingertips brushed the outer edge of Hannah's panties and she didn't say anything. The second sign was when she noticed Hannah very slightly open her legs a little but further apart, as if subconsciously giving her easier access.

"Hey Han, can I take the towel off? It makes it easier to massage the leg in one smooth motion. You got underwear on anyway, right?"

"Mmmm, that's fine." Hannah's voice purred out from under the table.

Chloe smiled, in relief more than anything, and took the towel off. Hannah was wearing some sheer black panties that were on the brink of being see-through. Chloe recognized them as one of the pairs Hannah had bought that day, and she found it curious as to why she decided to change. And this pair was considerably sexier than some of the others she had purchased. She put the thought to the back of her head and got back to the massage. She continued with the same stroke up the inner thighs all the way to the outer pussy lips. Hannah was clearly very relaxed and enjoying it, but Chloe wondered whether she was getting turned on. She got her answer soon enough when as her fingers were becoming braver and getting closer and closer to her Hannah's pussy, the movement caused her panties to become taught against her slit. When she moved her hands back, the panties came away slightly and clearly visible was a small wet patch. Chloe could again feel her heart in her chest and she thought about how to play this. Hannah was turned on but Chloe didn't want to risk ruining their blossoming friendship. She decided to ask her to turn over before she did something stupid.

Hannah turned over, barely opening her eyes, and as she did so mumbled, "God Chlo, it feels so good. Why did I wait so long for this?"

Chloe smiled and continued with her job starting again at the top. When she asked Hannah to turn around to avoid the danger of her becoming too turned on, Chloe hadn't considered that she now had Hannah's breasts to deal with. She began massaging the shoulders and chest and decided to continue as she would with a normal client, which is to spend a short amount of time on the breasts. When her hands brushed over her nipples for the first time, Hannah half opened her eyes and looked at her friend. "You having fun there?"

Chloe looked at her friend sweetly in the

eyes and said, "I'm working, Miss."

"Hmmm!" she had closed her eyes again but she was still smiling. Chloe continued to work her tits, watching her face the whole time. At one point, she noticed Hannah's tongue come out and lightly lick her lips. As she watched this Chloe was convinced that she could feel her own pussy begin to physically throb. She wished more than anything that she could bend down and give her a little kiss on the lips.

She moved down to the end of the table again and began to work the feet, massaging her way up to the ankles, calves, and thighs. She slid up her inner thighs and allowed her fingertips to lightly brush the edge of Hannah's panties. The wet spot that was visible before was growing, and Chloe knowing that Hannah was wet was finding it harder and harder not to touch her slit. Each time her hands glided up her legs, she let them go a tiny bit further. Chloe was watching both Hannah's face for signs of a reaction and also her chest, which she noticed was rising more and more prominently as though her breathing was getting deeper. Finally, after one upward motion, Chloe took her hands off of Hannah's skin and brushed her fingertips gently down over her pussy and back to her thighs. At the moment that her fingertips made contact with her pussy, she noticed Hannah take a sharp intake of breath. As she still hadn't said anything, Chloe decided to repeat this action a couple of times. By now, it was clearly no accident that she was touching her pussy and Hannah wasn't complaining.

Chloe decided to see how far she could push her and, using her thumbs, began to make circular movements up the inside of Hannah's legs all the way to the edge of her panties. Unlike previously, this time she decided not to stop here. She slid her thumbs inside Hannah's underwear and massaged her outer pussy lips. She heard Hannah moan and couldn't take it anymore. She slid her underwear down with one hand continuing to massage her pussy with the other. She could see her wetness now and Chloe needed more, she bent over and took one long lick from the bottom all the way to the top of her mound. She felt shivers run down Hannah's body, and she was now openly moaning. Chloe continued to lick and devour the pussy that she had been dying to taste since the first day the two girls met. When she looked up, she was staring into the eyes of the woman that she already knew she loved.

Hannah opened her eyes after giving in to the pleasure that her friend was giving to her as no man ever had before. As she looked into the same blue eyes that she had looked into with confusion so many times in the last few weeks, she felt nothing but love. Chloe continued to kiss and lick and suck on Hannah's pussy wanting nothing other than to give her friend the best orgasm she had ever had. She reached up and used her hands to massage her stomach and breasts. Each time she brushed past a nipple, she would pull at it and gently squeeze it under her fingertips. Each time she did it, Hannah would let out an involuntary moan and Chloe loved learning about what she enjoyed and reacted to.

As her breathing became even deeper and her hips were beginning to rise off the table, Chloe slowly and sensually brought her hands down Hannah's body and then let two fingers slip inside her cunt. She was so wet now; Chloe was having trouble licking it all up. She worked her fingers in and out of her pussy while her tongue focused on her sensitive clit. Chloe loved making her writhe around the table, and part of her wanted to tease her for longer. Another part of her though suspected that there would be plenty of time for teasing and knew that Hannah really needed to get off soon. She slipped another finger inside of her and began to massage the inside of her cunt while at the same time sucking her clit into her mouth. It only took a few moments of this before Hannah exploded and Chloe tasted the juices pouring out of her.

As she came down from her orgasm, Hannah found that she was suddenly overcome with emotion and wanted nothing but to kiss Chloe. She reached down and pulled her on top of her so they were both lying on the table. Hannah took Chloe's head in her hands and kissed her passionately on the lips. They both closed their eyes and enjoyed what they both knew be their first kiss of many. It was a while before Hannah broke the kiss and hugged Chloe close to her body, wishing that they could stay like that forever.

10 BATTLE OF THE HEART AND MIND PART 3

Lovers

Hannah woke up in Chloe's bed after having spent the night at her best friend's house. After weeks of denying and fighting her feelings for the out and proud Chloe, the previous day Hannah had finally given in to them. An innocent massage that Chloe offered to Hannah in order to help her painful back had quickly turned sensual and sexual. Up until that moment, Hannah had managed to control her feelings and keep them at bay, but when she had Chloe's hands all over her, she couldn't prevent her body's natural reaction. Chloe, of course, was aware of the way Hannah's body was responding to the massage, and when she saw her friend's pussy getting wet as a result of her hands, she couldn't help but find out how far she could take it. She started by using her fingers to tease Hannah's pussy and ended up licking her friend until she came hard.

Hannah sat up, looked next to her at the sleeping Chloe, and considered how beautiful she looked. As she looked at her soft peaceful face and her dark hair flowing onto the pillow, she felt a sudden rush of love and emotion sweeping over her body. It was a strange feeling that Hannah had never felt before. Hannah realized that her breathing had become labored and her feelings turned to nervousness and panic. What was going to happen when Chloe woke up? Did this signify a start to a new phase of their relationship? Did this make her a lesbian? Hannah felt as though the room was running out of oxygen and as though the walls were moving in towards her. With all of these questions going round and round in her head, all she wanted to do was get outside. Hannah ever so slowly lifted the blanket from off of her body and began to slide out of bed. The lifting of the blanket revealed one side of Chloe's naked body, and Hannah couldn't help but pause for a moment to take in the full beauty of the sleeping girl. Her smooth, tan skin had felt just as good as Hannah had remembered it looking that first day that they had met.

Hannah was battling with herself once again. The part of her that loved to look at her friend's naked form just wanted to slide back into bed and touch her all over one more time. But the other part was still struggling to believe that she had been licked and fucked by her best friend, a girl. "I'm not a lesbian," Hannah said in her head, as a means to push herself into repositioning the blanket over Chloe and quietly walking out of the bedroom. They had slept in Chloe's bedroom, but it had all started in the guestroom, where the professional masseuse kept her table and oils. Hannah walked into the room in search of her clothes, and as she saw the table and everything as they had left it, her mind flashed back to the previous evening and the events that had occurred here. She tried to figure out how it happened. It was just a massage. She had suspected in the past that Chloe was hoping their relationship would develop into something more than just friendship. When they had first met at the party, Chloe all but admitted that she was interested in Hannah. However, over the last few weeks as they had spent time together and become closer, Hannah never felt as though Chloe was up to anything or trying to take advantage. When the offer of a massage came up yesterday, it was purely professional and medicinal, in Hannah's mind anyway, and she was fairly sure that the case was the same for Chloe.

The truth is Hannah had found the massage arousing, but she was frightened to admit that, even to herself. The feeling of Chloe's hands on her body gave her pure pleasure. The whole time she had tried to just relax and think of the good it was doing for her tight muscles, but on a couple of occasions she had become aware of the sound of herself moaning. She knew that her pussy had become wet pretty early on in the massage and hoped that Chloe hadn't noticed. When she felt Chloe's hand begin to venture closer and closer to her pussy and her wetness, she couldn't deny that she wanted Chloe's hands to continue on their journey. By the time she had made contact with her pussy, Hannah was too turned on to fight it and simply allowed her body to get carried away in the amazing sensations. The aftermath of such a strong orgasm led to the couple hugging on the table until Hannah felt her eyes getting heavy and Chloe had led her off to the comfort of her bed. They had both drifted off to a peaceful and satisfied sleep with their arms wrapped around each other.

Hannah got dressed in silence, found her handbag, and let herself out of Chloe's apartment. As she walked down the street to the train station, she found herself wondering what Chloe would think and do when she woke up and found that Hannah was not there. Would she be angry? Or would she be relieved?

Suddenly it occurred to Hannah that she could be completely mistaken. She was worried sleeping with her would suggest to Chloe that she wanted to be in a relationship with her. But maybe Chloe would just see it as a one-time thing. Maybe now that she had slept with Hannah, she would have no interest in remaining friends with her. The thought of this made Hannah feel a little bit sick in her stomach. She loved Chloe, as a friend of course, or so she told herself. The thought of not seeing or speaking to Chloe everyday made Hannah feel as though she could cry. She took a deep breath and continued on her way, her mind a whirlwind of thoughts and emotions. "I'm not a lesbian," was the main recurring statement.

When Hannah's train arrived, she solemnly got on and found a seat. She thought about how happy she had been this last couple of weeks and considered if the reason was Chloe. When she deduced that it probably was, she reasoned with herself that everyone feels good when they make a new friend that they get on well with. But Hannah had to admit that throughout her relationship with Chloe, something had felt different than it did with other people. She couldn't put her finger on what it was. She just knew that she missed her when they weren't together, and she constantly had an overwhelming desire to be close to her. The one person that she wanted to ask to discuss what her feelings meant was the one person that she could not. She thought again about how Chloe would react when she woke up alone, closed her eyes, and hoped that she wouldn't be sad or angry. This reminded her of Chloe's smile, Hannah's favorite feature on her friend. She pictured her friends face and thought about how she would do just about anything to make her smile and happy.

Hannah noticed two girls sat down opposite and a few seats along. They had their hands on each other's legs and were talking quietly about something. They were both sitting along the edge, looking out the opposite window of the train but occasionally while they were talking, they would turn to look at each other and smile affectionately. Even from the distance between them and Hannah, she could see how happy they were and clearly in love. She looked again at their hands in each other's laps and thought how brave they must be to be so open about their relationship in public. When one of the girls glanced over and caught her looking, Hannah simply smiled shyly and looked away. She felt something in her heart and realized that she missed Chloe so much that it hurts. "If Chloe was here right now, I would hold her hand close to me too," Hannah thought as she stood up and waited for the doors to open as the train pulled up at her stop.

Hannah couldn't face going back to her empty apartment straight away, so she decided to walk around for a while. She wanted to get her head straight first and she knew once she got home she would feel lonely and sad. She had already considered on a number of occasions, calling Chloe to make sure she was ok. At one point, she took her phone out, found Chloe's name, and simply stared at the number on the screen. But what would she say when Chloe answers? Should she apologize? She put her phone back in her pocket deciding to leave it for a while. With time, it will be less awkward, she thought. It also dawned on her that Chloe would surely be awake by now and she hadn't tried to contact Hannah. She couldn't help feeling a little disappointed by that realization and wondered if one night really was all that Chloe had been interested in. She took her phone out again to double check that she didn't have any missed calls or messages but there was nothing. Hannah once again felt an unfamiliar feeling in her heart, and all she knew was that she didn't like it. Finally, she knew that it was time to head home where she could put on a film and pour herself a glass of wine to try and cheer herself up.

Hannah put her key in the lock and opened the door to her apartment. She walked inside with her head down and it was only when she had closed the door and taken a couple of steps inside that she looked around and saw it. Her apartment was filled with flowers. Red and white roses and flower petals decorated the floor, tabletops, and counters. Hannah slowly gazed around the room, trying to figure out what was going on. She heard a noise and turned around to see Chloe emerge from her bedroom holding yet another bouquet of flowers.

"Don't freak out, ok? I still have your spare key."

Hannah just stared in disbelief, still not sure what was going on. She opened her mouth but no sound came out. She didn't know what to say or do. So she just stood glued to the spot, staring at her friend.

Chloe took a few more steps forward, closer to Hannah. "I know you're freaking out about last night and that's normal. It was your first time with a girl and now you don't know what's going to happen."

Again, Hannah opened her mouth in attempt to respond but found that nothing happened. Chloe was still moving slowly further towards her, and Hannah found herself looking deep into the familiar dark blue eyes of her friend that managed every time to make her feel so safe and calm.

"But I want you to know how special last night was for me." Chloe took another step forward so now she was mere inches from Hannah. She was close enough that Hannah could smell her perfume and felt herself melt into the familiar feeling of her smell and her closeness. "I love you, Hannah."

Before she could answer, or really even take it all in, Hannah felt the soft warmth of Chloe's lips press lightly against her own. Her feet were still fixed to the spot but her eyes closed and she allowed herself to enjoy the kiss. Chloe gently moved her head back to look at Hannah. When she felt her lips move away, Hannah had an urge to follow them, not happy that the kiss was over so quickly. Chloe smiled, relieved to see Hannah's positive response and leant back in to continue the kiss. The kiss was soft and gentle for a few minutes while the girls enjoyed the taste and feel of each other's lips. Slowly it became more passionate with tongues slipping out to lick each other's lips and wrestle together in their mouths. Chloe dropped the flowers she was holding onto the floor, wanting her hands free to touch the other girls body. Hannah responded mutually and it wasn't long before they were pulling each other's clothes off.

"How about we do it in a bed this time?" Chloe joked, taking Hannah's hand and leading her, both naked, to the bedroom. Hannah had still not said a word since entering her own apartment but was secretly thankful to Chloe for taking the lead and for knowing Hannah better than she knew herself. She held tightly onto her best friends fingers and followed her into her own bedroom. In a similar style to the rest of the apartment, the bed was covered in flower petals. Hannah smiled and grabbed Chloe turning her around to continue kissing her. "Thank you," she whispered into Chloe's ear, just before Chloe pushed her onto the bed and climbed on top of her. She was so happy to have this opportunity again; she really had no idea how Hannah was going to react to her little surprise. Now she had her naked and in bed, she was going to make the most if it.

Chloe kissed down Hannah's neck and

loved that her friend immediately began to moan and nestle her neck closer to Chloe's mouth. When she reached Hannah's nipple, she felt her hips begin to gyrate against her hip, which was currently pressed up against Hannah's pussy. She could feel her wetness on her skin and loved that she was able to make her friend so hot. She continued on her way down the smooth milky skin of Hannah's stomach and kissed around her belly button. She moved down to lick and kiss the crease between her friend's thigh and mound. Hannah was getting increasingly turned on and increasingly wet and was now moving her hips trying to get Chloe's lips to make contact with her pussy faster. Chloe flicked her tongue in circles around Hannah's clit and it was driving her crazy. She took her hands and put them either side of Chloe's head directing her straight to her clit. She wasn't going to take any more of this teasing; she needed attention on her clit immediately. Luckily, Chloe was more than willing to give it to her. She sucked it into her mouth and held it gently between her lips as she shook her head from side to side. Hannah's moans were getting louder and more frequent, and Chloe could see her stomach muscles contracting. She kept the little nub in her mouth and used her tongue to gently flick over the tip of it, sending further sensations around Hannah's body. Chloe kept up the movement and it wasn't long before Hannah was squeezing Chloe's head between her knees as her body began to spasm into orgasm.

Chloe came up to kiss Hannah and she tasted her own pussy juices on her lips. Hannah wanted to make Chloe feel as good as she had made her feel so she pushed Chloe onto her back and then spun her body over to straddle her in the 69 position. Chloe smiled as she thought about the change in her friend who only that morning had sneaked out of her flat, too shy and ashamed to face up to the fact that she had slept with a girl. Now that same girl was kissing her pussy lips and wiggling her ass in Chloe's face. Chloe wasn't complaining; she grabbed Hannah's hips and pulled them down closer to her face. She stuck her tongue out and playfully gave Hannah's asshole a brief lick before diving her tongue into her wet pussy hole. When she felt her juices flowing, she switched it up, using her tongue to stimulate her clit again and inserting a finger into her cunt.

Hannah, who had never even kissed a girl before the previous evening, was enjoying her first taste of pussy. She was concentrating on what Chloe was doing to her at the other end of the bed and copying and imitating as much as possible. She was enjoying licking a girl's pussy more than she thought she would, and she loved it every time she felt Chloe twitch or heard her moan. All she wanted right now was to make her friend feel good. She alternated between flicking her tongue over Chloe's clit and making circles around her hole. She couldn't believe how good she tasted and thought how she would be happy to do this all day and night. When she felt Chloe put two fingers inside her hole, Hannah did the same thing. Both girls enjoyed this and were moving their hips back and forward and their fingers in and out in time with each other. Their moans also became synchronized, and as they got louder and louder, it was clear that both girls were going to come. Hannah found it hard to keep doing what she was doing as she felt her orgasm getting closer and closer. Chloe was also making it harder for her too as her hips were flying around as she began to spasm and find her nub too sensitive to be touched. Both girls screamed out as they finally finished and Hannah let her arms give way so she collapsed on top of Chloe. She tenderly kissed her friends thigh as they both came down.

Hannah turned her body around and went to lie on the bed next to Chloe, thinking excitedly about what else she had to learn about fucking a girl. She put her arm over Chloe's chest and gently kissed her cheek.

"I love you, Hannah." Chloe said still lying on her back and staring at the ceiling.

Hannah lifted herself up on one elbow to look at the other girl deeply and lovingly in the eyes. "I love you too, Chloe."

AUTHOR'S NOTE

Readers: I want to expand a few of the stories to see where the characters can be explored further. If there are any of the stories that you would like to read more about again, I'd love to hear from you!

Visit my blog at http://www.farrahseager.com

Join my newsletter for free exclusive previews
http://www.farrahseager.com/in

Follow me on Twitter at
http://www.twitter.com/farrahseager

Like my page on Facebook at
http://www.facebook.com/farrahseager

Discover my books at major ebook retailers everywhere.